Navigating
Customs

NAVIGATING CUSTOMS
NEW TRAVEL STORIES BY TWELVE WRITERS <25

**FEATURING ANOTHER TRESTLE CHAPBOOK
BY CLEO PASKAL**

**TENDRIL ANTHOLOGY SERIES
#3**

**EDITED BY
DANA BATH & TAIEN NG-CHAN**

Cumulus
PRESS
MONTRÉAL

Copyright © 2007 by Cumulus Press

Copyright of individual works, including those in the adjoining Trestle Chapbook, is maintained by their respective writers.

All rights reserved. No part of this book may be reproduced or transmitted in any form or by any means, electronic or mechanical, without the prior written consent from the publisher.

Dépôt légal, Bibliothèque nationale du Québec 2e trimestre 2007.
Legal Deposit, National Library of Canada 2nd quarter 2007.

Library and Archives Canada Cataloguing in Publication

Navigating customs : new travel stories by 12 writers under 25 / [edited by] Dana Bath, Taien Ng-Chan.

(Tendril anthology series ; bk. 3)
Includes a Trestle chapbook by Cleo Paskal.

ISBN 0-9733499-8-0
ISBN13 978-0-9733499-8-6

1. Travel–Fiction. 2. Short stories, Canadian (English). 3. Canadian fiction (English)–
21st century. I. Bath, Dana, 1970- II. Ng-Chan, Taien III. Paskal, Cleo IV. Series.

PS8323.T7N39 2007   C813'.010832   C2007-901351-1

Designed and typeset by Chester Rhoder @ Typo-pawsitive

Printed on **100% post-consumer recycled paper**
in Gatineau, Québec by **Imprimerie Gauvin**.

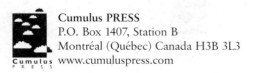

Cumulus PRESS
P.O. Box 1407, Station B
Montréal (Québec) Canada H3B 3L3
www.cumuluspress.com

To Joe and Sam Ollchan,
with whom I'd sail any ocean.

For my students, with whom I like to take small journeys,
and for Scott, with whom I wish to take many more.

CONTENTS

ANOTHER TRESTLE CHAPBOOK: #3
    The Medicine Woman of Butaritari   i (front flap)
BY CLEO PASKAL

PUBLISHER'S *Foreword*   eleven
EDITORS' *Introduction*   thirteen

AMY ATTAS (1985–)
    Sisters   seventeen

KARISHNA BOROOWA (1986–)
    Triptych   twenty-seven

RAFFY BOUDJIKANIAN (1984–)
    Catching Waves   forty-five

STACEY BOWMAN (1982–)
    Climb to the Sea   fifty-five

CHRISTINE ESTIMA (1981–)
    Between Berlin and Beirut   sixty-nine

AMY KLASSEN (1985–)
    White Girl Goes Deaf in Guyana   seventy-seven

SARAH-JEAN KRAHN (1984–)
    A Very Special Place — eighty-five

ALEX LESLIE (1984–)
    Bulls Coursed Through My Dreams All Night — ninety-five

ZARMINA RAFI (1982–)
    Of Travel and Art — one hundred and nine

FENN STEWART (1985–)
    Ya Idu, Blyad — one hundred and nineteen

GILLIAN SZE (1985–)
    Rooftop — one hundred and twenty-seven

TALIA WEISZ (1983–)
    Kupe's Voyage and Other Stories — one hundred and thirty-nine

ANOTHER TRESTLE CHAPBOOK (cont'd)
    The Medicine Woman of Butaritari — xiii
    BY **CLEO PASKAL**

ACKNOWLEDGEMENTS — one hundred and sixty-seven

PUBLISHER'S FOREWORD

THE TENDRIL ANTHOLOGY SERIES places the apprenticeship of new young writers under the age of 25 at the centre of Cumulus' publishing program. This third book in the anthology series—whose innovative book design includes a distinct but inseparable Trestle Chapbook by award-winning travel writer, Cleo Paskal—embodies its *raison d'être*: to provide a device for the mentorship of emerging writers from across Canada. Cleo's story is set aside within the French flap of the front cover in a format commonly used by the novice writer. This series attempts to eliminate the distinction between emergence and establishment because the latter is not possible without the former.

Taien Ng-Chan *has seen small parts of Australia, Canada, China, India, Nepal, Northern Europe, and the United States but her strangest and most recent journey was on a Dutch cruise ship across the Atlantic Ocean. She is author of* Maps of Our Bodies; *anthology editor of* Ribsauce; *reviews editor at* Matrix Magazine. *Her projects can be viewed at www.soyfishmedia.com.*

Dana Bath *has published two collections of short stories—*what might have been rain *(conundrum press) and* Universal Recipients *(Arsenal Pulp)— and one novel,* Plenty of Harm in God *(DC Books). She has won a number of literary awards. Bath is originally from Corner Brook, Newfoundland, and now teaches English Language and Literature at Vanier College in Montréal. She used to travel a lot, and one day will again.*

Editors' Introduction

IN MY ENGLISH 101 classes, we often read Alistair MacLeod's "The Boat." In this story, the narrator's mother and father have lived in the same village their whole lives. His mother is afraid of anything and anyone outside the village; his father is determined that his son should seek an education and see the world. When we discuss why the father has such a different worldview than the mother, my students point out that the father, when he is not working, is reading. He cannot explore the world, and yet he can explore the world. He can't travel, and yet, in his every free moment, he is traveling.

I also teach a course on travel literature. We read portions of "Voyage Around My Room," written by Xavier de Maistre as he served forty-two days under house arrest. De Maistre writes a travelogue about his bedroom, detailing the adventures he has there and the particularities of the environment in which those adventures unfold. One of my students' assignments is to write a travel piece about a place in which they spend a lot of time: their workplace, the college cafeteria, the Montréal subway. Reading these pieces, I get to travel into their worlds and see things I never see in my own, or travel to places I go to every day and notice them for the first time.

Reading and writing are traveling experiences. As readers, we enter worlds that are unfamiliar; our perceptions are challenged or illuminated; we see our thoughts and experiences reflected in a new context, the context of the writer's mind. As writers, we try to view our own worlds with fresh eyes, the way a traveller does, or we try to imagine and capture a world unlike our own. In all cases, we are trying to find the known in the unknown and vice versa. This is what traveling is, and what it is for. Traveling, in all its forms, makes us bigger.

Having finished reading these stories, I envy you, reader, the journey ahead. It will be different for you than it was for me, as a story is as much about the reader as a voyage is about the traveler. Regardless, you, like me, will be bigger when you're done. And you, like me, will carry what you find here away with you as you leave, like a pocket full of souvenirs. — **DANA BATH**

FOR SOME PEOPLE, THE urge to travel is irresistible; for others, it is only out of necessity that they go anywhere. And there are as many reasons to travel as there are types of travellers. People travel to visit family, to go to work, to be on vacation, to run away from something, to see other places and meet other people. There are thoughtful travellers, boorish travellers, and tourists.

What exactly is the difference between a traveller and a tourist? It used to be much easier to make this distinction. The tourist stayed on the beaten path and saw the sights from a safe distance; the traveller sought to erase the distance, to find the authentic experience. But in our increasingly small world, where can one go that has not already been gone to thousands of times over, that hasn't turned into a tourist commodity? The old differences

Editors' Introduction

between travellers and tourists are blurring, as unstable as borderlines on a world map.

Nowadays, the only really authentic mode of travel depends on your state of mind. To travel is to expand your awareness about your own being and your otherness, as well as your relationship to your surroundings. This part, I think, is the key difference between tourism and travel. To travel is not just about recreation. It is necessarily to navigate customs, not just by crossing borders, but by confronting local traditions.

The stories in Navigating Customs explore the whole range of travel and genre, from backpacking to foreign aid work to family visits, and from short fiction to creative non-fiction to poetry. But the main thing that links all these works by young authors is their awareness and their sensitivity in portraying the journeys of themselves or their characters. They strive to be thoughtful travellers, even when they play the part of tourist.

You could be riding the city bus in Montréal or on a tourbus in Thailand. You could be walking around the familiar neighbourhood in which you grew up, or lost somewhere in the tangled streets of Amsterdam or Kathmandu. Wherever you are, you become a traveller when you slow down, to really look, smell, listen, think. Travel isn't just about where you are going. It's about the experience of the journey, with all of its accompanying discoveries, disjoints and discomforts. You see things differently on the journey, which is there for you even when you don't cross a border, and the customs you navigate are your own.

— **TAIEN NG-CHAN**

*If **Amy Miriam Sturton Attas** wasn't such a laid-back baby, she would have been named Anna. Instead, she was best friends with her. Amy considers the tiny wilderness town of Pinawa, Manitoba, her home, but she's currently studying English and Creative Writing at York University in the endless concrete of Toronto. She has traveled Canada coast to coast and seen Greece, Costa Rica, Kenya, England (for eight hours, between flights), Germany and Nicaragua. She dreams of biking from Alaska to Chile on the Pan-American highway and sauntering to the North Pole with nothing but a pair of snowshoes and a pen. She's planted over 100,000 trees, played over one hundred University hockey games, torn one ACL and lost her passport twice.*

SISTERS

THERE IS A COW in front of me. She doesn't care that the mud clinging to the hairs on her spine has ruined her silk coat. She doesn't mind that she eats garbage, and will not acknowledge any idiot taking pictures of her protruding rib cage. She is a Kenyan cow. Of course she doesn't mind. I lower my camera. A spindly man bouncing by on a bicycle shouts, "Jambo! Pic a picture!" his torso twisted and arm stretched back so I will indulge him. I return his bleached smile and make a show of focusing the camera before pressing my finger down next to the shutter release. I will not waste my film on boys, especially ones who greet me with the tourists' "jambo" instead of the locals' "habari". I'll take my time with my friend Heifer and walk to town.

I feel more alone today than I have in weeks. I know why, but I'm not letting myself think about it. I should focus on the present. I should savor the experience.

I am in Africa working in small town orphanages, the only female caring for hundreds of motherless children. There are always other women around kneading pounds of chapatti dough or hunched over basins of laundry, but no one else seems to pay attention to the kids. Even the other female volunteers spend more time in town buying sweets for the orphans than actually working.

The stray souls we teach have dust on their skin, urine on their clothes and dried pus flaking off sores on their shaved heads; I do too, less the pus, after living the small-town Kenyan life. The flies from the television infomercial even land on my face (I don't have a personal assistant to blow them away while cameras roll). This altruism may seem feminine, but I know plenty of men who have chosen a life like mine. You don't need two X chromosomes to understand that the nine-year-old who looks like a three-year-old needs those chapattis more than he needs a stick of gum.

Besides, I've never been convinced I am a girl. When you stack up all the evidence, it's pretty clear I'm female, but still, I wonder. There are mornings when sleep clings and I wake up not entirely convinced it's Friday, or Thursday, or whatever day it's supposed to be, and that's how I feel about my sex. I wish I could get immersed in the world but I can't stop staring at the scratch on the lens that reminds me I'm not involved. Like people from Southern Ontario who try to speak French, I force a delay into every reaction. But everyone else seems to believe the evidence, and so I act as a woman.

In high school I had a friend named Toiny, who, to me, epitomized femininity (a word I even have trouble pronouncing). In my group of friends, she was always the first to compliment me if I wore a dress and let me experiment with her huge boxes of make-up, and she was also the first one the guys noticed. At basketball tournaments they'd ask me what number four's name was; at dances they'd say Hi to Toiny and walk by the group around her. At summer camp they grinned as they struggled to say Toy-knee without even asking who I was. We'd bug her about the endless tail of boys flapping behind her and she claimed she hated it. I always thought she was lying.

Being Toiny in high school is like being white in Africa. My walk to town winds through stacks of apartments where children sit drawing pictures in the dirt. When I walk by they never fail to scuttle behind, shouting, "How are you How are you," not even taking breath for a question mark. It's the only English most of them know. When I answer "I'm fine thank you, how are you?" they stand as still as a broken-down safari truck, awed. The dust they've kicked up in their rush through the street has time to settle on the ground. In town the shopkeepers hiss, selling lies and over-priced postcards to every mzungu. They ask my name so they can tell me theirs; they give me phone numbers so they can have mine. I tell them, in Swahili, "Don't give me the white-woman's price, I'm a volunteer," but every day it's the same battle. At first sight men tagged Toiny as a beauty worth catching. Locals tag me as a gullible, English-speaking tourist in even less time.

The kids at the orphanage are continually amazed at the attention I get around town. We even make up a game of tag where they crawl all over me, worshiping the mzungu, then run away laughing and screaming when I start to roar. I pinch myself every time I get these kids to smile and live in the moment. Years of worry wash away when they're finally convinced that they're taken care of, that they're loved.

People followed Toiny. Growing up, everyone walking to school from the east side of my town cut across the same field to save time. In summer, the grass was worn to dirt and bedrock. In winter, one hundred shoes packed the flakes after every snowfall. Toiny was the first to cross the smothered field the morning after a blizzard and I watched as she trudged forward, plowing a crooked path. In summer we could have picked a straighter route, but in snow up to our knees no one else was willing to get their sneakers wet. We took her path for two weeks, and everyone arrived at school five seconds later than they could have. Toiny didn't even remember carving the path, let alone realize the snowballing effects of the precedent she'd set.

People followed me, too, but I didn't notice, didn't care, or freaked out. In Grade Nine I went to prom dressed in neon orange pants and my grandpa's blue plaid suit jacket. My hair was short, green, and spiked. I went to the dance with Jason Wilson, a boy in Grade Ten who was well-liked but not overly popular. While we slow-danced with our elbows locked and our arms straight, he asked me out. Like, you know, that boyfriend/girlfriend thing. I should have seen it coming. Obvious Hint #1: he'd asked me to another dance earlier in the year (I couldn't go because of a basketball tournament). Obvious Hint #2: who asks a girl to a high school dance without intending to ask her out? But I couldn't believe that anyone followed

Sisters

me. I refused him. I said I wasn't ready. Ready for what? Telephone conversations about *The Simpsons*? Holding hands? Maybe a French kiss three weeks in?

I cried that night and for four years afterwards. It wasn't that I wished I'd said yes to Jason, but that I wondered why I'd said no. Saying no brought up more questions than I could deal with as a teenager. Why I was unwilling to commit to anybody. Why, when I'd finally been recognized as a girl, I refused.

A year later, Jason died of a rare birth defect. Six months after that, I learned of another guy who had been interested in me. Jason's death wasn't hard because of the loss of life (I didn't know him well enough for that), but because of the loss of opportunity. Now that he's gone, I can never go back and tell him how chicken I was. My girl friends did not help me cope with these losses. I was not ushered into a womb of sage advice and old wives' tales. Experiencing the extremes of girlish trauma did not allow me to forge new links with the women in my life. I keep getting this email forward that says all women are sisters, but I've never felt like I was part of that club. What a rip-off.

But like our lives, this story is not finished yet. I am still not a woman.

I wish I were more like the tall, slender, elegant giraffe. A biological anomaly, and yet world-renowned for grace and style. Not only does the giraffe reach heights none of its competitors can to find food, but she attacks the plants no other herbivore would dare touch. The acacia tree is too menacing for the gazelle and impala, who are tempted by its clusters of leaves but can't navigate its many thorns. The giraffe's tongue can wrap around an acacia branch taking only the prize, and even if she slips and swallows a thorn it will pass through her system unnoticed. Yes, sometimes I wish I were a giraffe. All that faultless execution and poise when things don't go as planned.

When I was fifteen I shaved my head as an experiment in human psychology. I received wild support from everyone in my town. Bald heads attract hands, and many women touched mine with veneration and pride. But outside of my sheltered home where people knew less of my personality, the same old issues were brought into question again. At a Pizza Hut just off the highway in Northern Ontario, the waitress served each of us our first slice. But when I held up my plate, she pushed it away saying, "ladies first." In Toronto, after I helped a paper-pushing Christian propagandist get onto the right subway train, she crouched beside me and asked "Are you a boy or a girl?" and then, "That's what I thought," when I enlightened her. These women aren't my sisters. I don't know why I let them off so easily, choosing to slouch in my own embarrassment instead of pushing them into their own. I could have flashed my breasts at the pizza waitress to prove a point. I could have answered "both" to the Christian. But I didn't. Just like I hold back in Kenya.

I brought a cotton sundress with me to Africa that I've worn since I was thirteen. Needless to say, by North American standards it is not risqué. All the guidebooks warn female travelers to avoid tank tops, keep skirts below the knee and tuck in tees (men are fine in underwear, apparently). As I walk to town photographing Heifer and other Kenyan oddities, I'm wearing this sundress for the first time, with a men's dress shirt to cover my shoulders. I hear men calling "Mzungu!" from across the street. When kids call me a mzungu it's tolerable; with adults it's derogatory. Heifer hangs back in the outskirts of town, knowing the dangers a girl like her faces amidst roaring diesel engines and eyes that see too little. I walk on alone. The man selling newspapers calls me beautiful, emphasizing every syllable. I keep my head low and watch the fluttering papers held down by shards of glass, then walk on. The brothers selling used watches reach out to the edge of the sidewalk to get my attention and push a fake Timex onto my hip. Its gold strap is worn down to steel and the lens is scratched. I look the other way and keep moving.

I step into the street to reach the internet café. There is a man crossing in the other direction whose eyes won't leave mine. I try to look away. Other people are hurrying to cross through this break in traffic, and as I try to find room for my white-sandaled feet, I catch his gaze again. I swerve in my path to avoid bumping into him, but he matches my steps and passes right beside me. We rub shoulders. His hand grasps my thigh, rubs up to my waist and threatens to go between my legs before we separate.

I pull down on my skirt and turn towards him with my mouth open. Is this normal? Should I shout? Can I punch him in the face without getting arrested? My connections to what is normal are limited when I'm in my own culture, but what is a man allowed to do to a woman in Africa? Like a tourist fascinated with an African advertisment, I stand in the middle of the street as the gap in traffic rapidly closes. "The river of cars stops for no one," I had been warned on my first day in Kenya. I stagger backwards, still gripping my skirt with one hand, now closing my dress shirt with the other. A truck roars by, slapping my hair into my face. The man looks back to me with an open smile on his face as he struts away. He wants to make sure I know his fluttering hands moved with intent. I wouldn't have been surprised if he'd winked.

My friend got malaria and had to fly home last week. We took the pills, we slept under nets, we wore bug spray even though we never saw mosquitoes. Sometimes there's nothing you can do to stop bad luck from striking. I was going to the café to write her an email that said I was still having fun, but I missed her. I was going to write that impossible note that lets her stop worrying without getting jealous. Last night I tried to call her from the payphone below my apartment, but a sixty-year-old drunkard from the bar across the street pushed his cell phone at my chest until I had to lock myself inside. Now at least I have a story to prove how I miss her. Dear Anna, how do you punish sexual assault?

So I do have friends, and I've made more in Africa. Girls I have more in common with than matching chromosomes. I hear Toiny's working at a bar now that boasts busty waitresses. Every Saturday night the owners set up a runway and have all their employees strut in lingerie. It's amazing how people explode out of small-town high school stereotypes, or take them to profitable extremes.

These days the men must trail her in droves. I wonder if she feels more like a woman.

I walk home from the café using a different route that winds through a peaceful Indian neighbourhood free from honking, prowling matatus. I see my girl Heifer and she snorts knowingly as I pass. My shirt is buttoned up to the collar. Instead of the banners advertising Christian revivals that drape the other road out of town, I slip under trees that look like Canadian Maples. I slow my pace to match the shuffle of a shriveled Punjabi woman up ahead so I don't have to pass. Old wise men get the title 'mzee' in Swahili. I wonder what the women are called.

Two young men zip up on bicycles and wave at me, shouting, "How are you, Mzungu!" I raise a hand even though they've already passed—I know their eyes are still on me. The woman in front of me turns slowly to see who's getting all the attention. I raise my limp body and catch her stare, but she doesn't look away. "Habari," she says. Her voice is like the womb. I have been waiting six weeks to use the local's reply. "Mzuri," I respond. Mine is not the infant's cry.

NAVIGATING CUSTOMS

Karishma Boroowa *is a second-year Political Science student at the University of Ottawa. She began writing fiction in English in Grade Nine, encouraged by her mother Archana Medhi and also by her teacher, Ms. Anahita Lee. Karishma is multilingual, and loves art, travelling, fencing, thinking, and eating Tandoori prawns.*

TRIPTYCH

I

Kari

I HAVE ALWAYS BEEN fascinated by the diversity of Hindu Gods, the portraits of whom abound in my Grandmother's apartment. Dressed in bright ornate robes of vermilion, turquoise, gamboge and emerald green, and sporting chains and chains of jewellery, they are a striking contrast to the cool shades and the sleek sofa set in the living room. I often begin to point it out to my Grandmother, but then stop. After all, even though she said she could make straighter lines if given a wooden ruler, she still hung that Piet Mondrian print right above the sleek sofa, the lines of which go so well with the room. Unfortunately, the effect of change, of making it an urban chic, failed miserably. A clutter of odds and ends arranged very, very neatly, but still clutter, gives the room a cottage-like feel. In the living room, right in the centre on top of the plush dove-grey carpet, is a huge and lavishly carved wooden statue of Ganesha the elephant God, or rather the half-human, half-elephant Hindu God of Prosperity and Luck. When my Grandmother told me the myth of Lord Ganesha, I patted the smooth potbelly and figured that he got lucky his Father found an elephant and not a lizard in the forest.

The tale of Ganesha starts when Goddess Parvati, Lord Shiva's consort, makes a handsome clay figure of a strong youth. She breathes life into her creation and there he stands, arms akimbo, keeping guard while Parvati bathes. She specifically tells him to not let anyone disturb her during her bath. I always used to wonder why and who did she think would disturb her, surely, not her eager, passionate husband? So, the youth stands guard, while Parvati's husband returns and demands to see his wife. Not realizing that this man might be his Father, Parvati's creation attacks the Lord, at which point the enraged and unbelieving Lord Shiva decapitates him. "Off with his head!" Grandmother's private joke until I grew up enough to wince every time French Revolution and Hindu myth mixed together.

Meanwhile, the lovely Goddess Parvati, dishevelled and damp, hurries outside to find out the cause of all this hullabaloo. Her eyes nearly pop out with shock and her husband gets the "correct it or you will get the cold shoulder for eternity ultimatum." When one is a Hindu God there is a double dilemma. Firstly, Hindu Goddesses are extremely beautiful and buxom beings, and secondly, who knows what a female's conception of eternity means?

I add on necessary blood and gore when I retell it to my children. This generation-upon-generation old story has to at least match up to the newest flick, with just the right amount of romance to be "Ewww..." and lots of Batman-

Triptych

style pop-ups of wham-bam-slam, with heads flying, blood pouring and bones crunching. I tuck in my youngest whose eyes are drooping, there they go, almost.

"So, Lord Shiva (like all harassed husbands) promises to replace the decapitated head with the head of the first living creature that comes along." The poor elephant, it was It. (Where did the first head, the human head go? Why could not that be used? I hate it when myths leave loose ends.)

"...and the great big elephant, with the two formidable tusks, sacrificed its head so that the youth, who would now be known as Lord Ganesha, could live again."

Miraculously revived by Lord Shiva, Lord Ganesha would henceforth bring prosperity and luck to all households. Whatever it might be that makes my adult mind regurgitate the story in a much different way than the folk-artsy way my Grandmother told it, part of me still wants to believe in the awesome supernatural powers of such Gods. My credulity can encompass it. Otherwise it is just too scary to believe that I am in total control of my life, for who else is there to blame if not the Fates and God?

Yesterday, when the children were playing, they chipped the old Ganesha statue. I had to rush to Wal-Mart and get super-glue. Fix the God before Grandmother puts on the spectacles and creates after-dinner fireworks by blaming it solely on me. "Your house is never clean and can you not manage the kids from breaking the little possessions I have?" How she can string in three totally unrelated criticisms is beyond me.

Later, that evening, she comes in wearing a purple saree. Royalty colour, a warning sign? I can hardly eat my dinner. I know it is foolish to worry about a broken God fixed with super-glue. I am an adult, but I am still worrying about the statue. I hope the piece stays stuck for she does have the ability to rob me of my dignity-inducing years. She slowly takes her seat at the table, and it is slow; she has arthritis, and I await the shriek-fest. I have no idea how she makes her English sound so husky and our mother tongue so shrieky. I meet her eyes, waiting and waiting.

Ultimately, the Fates have the last laugh. All that perspiration for nothing. She hugs the children Good-night and walks the long length to the elevator.

"O, Kari, I noticed the Ganesha…"

Mental gasp!

"Right, but it was…"

She is speaking over my words "It shifted a bit off centre, I had to ask Lok-bhai to move it, bad for my back."

"Really? Good night then."

Do I thank God or Man for the way the elevator doors shut so fast?

Triptych

II

Maya

"Should I get a new one?" I ask my daughter.

Kari is busy washing the dishes. She frowns and distractedly says, "What? Mother, really, can't you see..."

I interrupt, "I'm talking about the Ganesha, should I get a new one while I'm in Kathmandu?"

Silence.

"Since I'm going to Rashmi's, will be able to find something in Janakpur if not near the airport in Kathmandu."

"How did you know?" her eyes scowl at me. I smile, let her guess, I say.

Ten, Eleven-ten, Twelve-two, One-twenty, Two-ten, Three-five, Four-thirty, Five, Six, Seven-twenty, Eight-ten, Nine, Ten, Eleven-fifteen, Twelve. Finally, I scream to myself in silent relief, *Nepal*.

There we were, riding a bumpy ride, up and down, through curves and rolls, synclines and more synclines, round and round a terrible roller-coaster trip to Janakpur. I have been shifted to the younger nephew's car by a very grateful elder nephew. Really now, if it were my daughter Kari or my Mother here, they would thank all their assorted deities that it is I who am making this trip.

"Go on, go and hug your Maya Grand-Auntie," that is Rashmi's daughter prodding her son. An audible "don't want to." Another Grandniece comes and hands me a bouquet of flowers and then quickly runs back and hides behind her mother's saree. I take the spicy-sour bites of tittora from my bag and stretch it towards them. "Say thank you," another agitated whisper follows more forceful prodding. The children remain glued.

The next day I have an easier time. On one of those never-ending steep roads I see a passel of monkeys near a little shrine. I interrupt Nephew Number Two in the middle of his monologue and ask him to stop the car. "Whose shrine is it?"

"Hanuman-ji's."

I take my camera out and begin clicking pictures. Kari's children would love them. There is an adorable mother and child monkey duo. I approach them cautiously. They are clustered near a huge Banyan tree, the roots of which provide Tarzan-like swings for the brethren. Nearby older, and I guess male monkeys, feed on offerings left by mothers, daughters and wives who visit the temple regularly.

It gets hot. I send my Nephew for cups of chai, good to be old, have the youngsters do the work.

"Auntie, will we be here long?"

Triptych

"Aren't there just so many monkeys?"

"It is the Hanumanji temple, the monkey God has to have his faithful, no?"

Our first conversation. I believe we are making progress. I abstractedly look around. A bit of evolution from those monkeys, I think, but how did our eyes get that unique lift at the edges, a different species of monkeys was it? I look at the concentric circles that top into a spire with a red flag blowing from it. Strange though, the only Hanuman story I remember is him crossing India to Sri Lanka, and setting Lanka on fire.

I drink the syrupy sweet chai. "So, after shopping, do we have anything to do?"

"We are having a Puja in the afternoon, at two Auntie, Raku got the new house and we have to hold the household ceremonies. We got the regular Pundit too, the same one who has memorized the entire Sanskrit verses and last year, he conducted all our religious ceremonies so well. It will be a two-in-one thing, we won't have to hold the Saraswati puja after two days then."

"Hmm... Hmm... And lots of people?"

"Just the family and maybe the neighbours."

"That's a lot, eight households surround you and if I remember correctly, consider the..."

"Yes, yes Auntie, but it's not too many, just the children and grandparents will come and maybe a mother or two.

Fathers will come only for eating the prasad, long after the ceremonies are over."

"Can you hold my camera, I will just throw the cup in the bin."

"Leave the camera here, everyone does it."

I walk over to the bin, and then hear a shriek and much laughter nearby. I see my nephew gesticulating at the tree.

"Eiyee...what are you doing? Throw it down, throw it down..." my nephew is alternately pleading and commanding.

"My camera! You horrible monkey!" and there my curses follow. Nephew looks horrified. I do not know if it is because of the monkey or me. "Give it back, you dumb ass." The chai server and the men are laughing. "Shut up you all, make the monkey give it back!" The hullabaloo of the entire crowd chases the monkeys away. They leave with an expensive present—my camera—and a flick of red buttocks. I glare at my nephew who has gone through such a gamut of emotions, from shock to horror to amusement to chagrin that he is speechless. I want to scream at him, but I feel lost among the cheery faces, for my predicament seems funny to all those who thank heaven and earth that the same thing didn't happen to them.

I return in a foul mood, whatever concord I had with Nephew Number Two is long gone. He is happy to shuttle me off to Nephew One, who informs me that I must wear a saree to the Puja, but "I haven't got one."

Triptych

"What do you mean you haven't got one?"

The priest, the same one I remember, comes wearing a white loincloth with a yellow scarf around his neck. He removes his shirt and pats the Brahmin's thread firmly into place. How can he be comfortable showing off his potbelly? Four white lines smear his forehead with a red dot stroked at its centre.

"I want to go to the loo, Mahi." The children suddenly flock towards Rashmi.

I wonder what Rashmi will do with these children. They fidget in the heat. Dressed up in finery and imitation jewellery, they squat in a semi-circle behind the priest. A few are caught up in their clothes, unable to sit, stuck as they are with huge safety pins, hairpins and all sorts of adhesives. I hear a few ominous rips as they shuffle into place. I wave at Loona and Lisa, the sisters, and make my way towards them. Thank all the million Hindu deities that the old timers get the chairs! Rashmi has given me a chunni to cover my head with. She still disapproves of my jeans. "From abroad," she whispers to her cohorts. They nod while smiling at me.

"Gyanit samajh gyami, pushpanit samajh gymai," the priest intones, convoluted Sanskrit words boring me. I bet the children cannot understand a word either. My minimal Sanskrit could not keep up with the wide variety of changes each word goes through in terms of first, second, third persons, gender and plurality. The priest then makes us all stand while he screams "All the Gods?"

Everyone shouts, "Hail!"

"All the demons?"

"Destroy!"

A bit more of that prepared dialogue; the children love the shouting bit, gives them a vent for their frustration. Then Rashmi, as the lady of the house, puts the earthen lamps in front of the priest who blesses them. In turn, we take the blessings of those blessed lamps by sweeping the air above it with our hands and transferring that caught air over our hair. Meanwhile, the children are already in line, waiting for the prasad. I cannot see why they should be enthused about foods that my doctor recommends. There are sprouts, chick peas mixed with a sharp lemon, sweet coconut paste, cut bananas with their peel on and oxygenated apples. This entire spread of prasad is served on a banana leaf, picked from one of the plants that lines Rashmi's veranda.

I like the heavy coconut smells, the incense and jasmine that the Puja brings. At the same time, I cannot help but feel conflicted. It is not that I do not believe in God, I do, but I do not know what to think about the ceremonies we undertake. One part of my mind finds it irrational, hypocritical, a bribe, and a waste of time and money. The other part of me, the fanciful part of me, wants to believe that it will really invite the Gods to our house. That gets me wondering what form they would take on if they came for a visit. Would it be a human shape, or that of an animal? Would they come as a shaft of light, a voice from thunder and clouds, or would they be invisible? I cannot grasp the

Triptych

concept of it, I do not understand what I would want God or the Gods to do or say. I glaze over at the eyes and go off into tangents, thoughts and daydreams.

Luckily, ginger wine relieves me of those. Lisa walks towards me saying "Didn't think you would come, did we Loona?" I smile and we eagerly exchange gossip, bargaining piece by piece for each juicy detail. I tell them about the Ganesha too. "Oh, I know what you are talking about, Rashmi has the twin. Just go past the vestibule till you reach the puja room."

"Am I going to filch it and somehow stuff it into my suitcase?" I ask petulantly.

"Don't be silly, would we wish all that bad karma on you? Just replace it. Get Rashmi one of those extra huge Ganeshas with semi-precious stones and with real clothes stitched onto it and you can take…"

"How much do you think it will be?"

"Come on, you earn in dollars, you can afford to spend in rupees."

We all laugh, but mine is a bit strained. Kari will have to take the brunt of the expenses.

Soon, Nephew Two says, "Auntie, have a safe journey."

"Yes, thank you for the Ganesha."

"Don't mention it, we couldn't have two such huge statues in our house, one would get jealous of the other."

NAVIGATING CUSTOMS

Nephew Number Two cries plaintively "Do I have to carry it?"

"Consider it punishment for the lost camera."

Ten, Eleven-ten, Twelve-two, One-twenty, I sleep and dream of to-do-lists, Three, Three is a magic number I think, me, Kari and my Mother... Five, Six, Seven-twenty, Eight-ten, Nine, Ten, Eleven-fifteen, Twelve. Finally, I scream to myself in silent relief, *Canada*.

III

Mother

"Mrs. Medhi, I must tell you that those extra pounds really put weight on your knee."

"Yes, yes, will have her put on..." Maya hurriedly butts in.

Really now, I interrupt, "Maya, I can speak for myself."

"It's not that, Mother, but..."

"So, I would strictly advise you to join a walking club, or you could even come here to..." the Doctor's cool voice seemingly unconcerned about our private disputes.

Just to unbalance the Doctor, I say triumphantly, "That's not going to happen."

Triptych

"Really now, Mrs. Medhi, I must advise..."

"Doctor, I understand, I just meant I won't come here to..."

Maya suddenly interrupts with a brilliant idea, according to the doctor. For me it means getting up at six o'clock on a spring morning, when it is so dark that it feels like three. I sulk the entire journey back home. Then I set up a calendar that counts the days until the hour of my physical reckoning.

On the fated Thursday morning, I quickly don my loosest salwar suit, borrow Kari's comfortable Skechers and prepare myself for my soon-to-be weekly torture. I am beginning to think that Maya really took that doctor's prattle seriously. Suddenly, the whine of the phone echoes into the silent room. I pick up the phone. "Hello?"

A squeaky voice pipes in. "Oh, Auntie, a bit late I know, just wanted to know if you arrived home safely?"

"What?" I wonder, and realize the message is for Maya.

"Oh, it's you then, I meant Auntie Maya, and how are Kari and the children..."

It sounds suspiciously like Nephew Two, back in Nepal. Maya's story didn't endear him much to me.

"Get the time difference and call later." I hang up.

The watch says that it is barely seven. The Westons soon pick me up with sleepy Good-Mornings and we silently wind up the narrow driveway until we reach Sharma's place.

"Hello, hello!" So buoyant, it is downright ghastly. "Fine morning, come to the balcony." We all troop inside and then we are outside again. The Paintals, Pinny and Toby, are already there.

"Yes, yes, we are nearly all here. Kiran might not make it, though that is going to mean extra strain on her back, and she already has so many problems, poor thing." I think I am going to be next on the hit list, so I quickly walk down till the end. "Take your position behind your mat and let us begin," and so begins my first yoga class.

I have no idea how some of them manage to contort their bodies. Mr. Sharma is praising Toby. "Bloody show-off," I mutter. Just because he cannot see himself, looking like a turned-over grasshopper... I glance around and stop my grumbling. It just would not do to let them think I needed some mental exercise too.

Now they are cleaning their respiratory passages or something. I exclaim disgustedly. A fat straw has been shoved through one nostril and into the mouth. I refuse to attempt it and glance around with horrified fascination. Water is sucked out from one end and blown out through the other. The beginning and the end are alternated through each of the respiratory orifices. Everyone is doing it! Just because Mr. Sharma said so. I have to look away, looks like it is going to be my last yoga class.

Triptych

Kari picks me up. She is not as straight about it as Maya. Hesitantly, she says "So, are you coming again?"

"No."

"Oh, but Mother said..."

"Maya can say what she wants."

"But..."

"I know about the Ganesha. I cannot tell you how much..."

"No, really, it was a..."

"Don't interrupt me."

"No, but..."

I override her. "I can use it as leverage. Maya tripped over it and broke it, you know. She strategically placed it, but I noticed, so..."

"No!"

"What? I just said..."

"No, and all this time I had thought the children had..."

"What are you babbling about? And you know what, it suddenly healed. Miracles happen but not like this."

Kari suddenly laughs hysterically. Maybe it is a gene thing, we have those moments an awful amount of times.

Back home, I have a deliciously cool bath and get ready for the morning worship. I purse my mouth and blow the conch. A lovely booming sound reverberates across the walls. Will the neighbours wake up? Maya comes, bringing the flowers with her. "Robbed the neighbour's garden." I roll my eyes at the accumulated bad karma and offer prayers to even the balance. I light the incense sticks and fan the lit coconut coir until the rope smokes. We have to put it under water soon or the fire alarms will ring. A balance between worship and fire safety has to be reached too. Kari would go ballistic if she saw all these fire hazards. We both kow-tow before the deities that line the worship-room and in front of the powerful blue-skinned and peacock-feather-adorned Lord Krishna we pray. Maya then lights three earthen lamps, one for me, one for Kari and one for herself. The light burns steadily on as we kneel-walk away. A brilliant morning awaits us.

Raffy Boudjikanian *is a finishing journalism and political science student at Concordia University. He has grown up in Canada though he is of Armenian descent from Lebanon. He hopes to build a successful career in journalism and long-form fiction and non-fiction writing. He lives in Montréal with his family. Raffy enjoys traveling and has seen much of Western Europe and Armenia. Last summer he combined his love for trips with his journalistic curiosity for a stay in Nicaragua.* Catching Waves *is the story of how he almost never returned.*

CATCHING WAVES

THE OCEAN LAPS UP all the way to my knees. Apparently old black leather shoes and khaki pants suit its taste, because next I am swallowed whole.

My eyes burn. My heart thumps. My hands frantically search for something to hold. Miraculously, they find it. My face is flattened against a mighty stone, which I grip as hard as I can, letting the waves of the Pacific wash over me. I pray for the strength to not let go. Visions of being carried away and then hurtled back on the boulders at the bottom of the cliff - a bloody mess - dance in my mind. I hold my breath as the enormous pressure pulls at me. Each passing moment is one more chance for my strength to fail.

The water at last retreats. My aching fingers would have me believe the incident lasted hours, though my mind tells me it could not have been more than a few seconds. I back up quickly, as far toward the bottom of the rocky cliff as I can. This would not do. If those waves had been that high and strong, the next ones would definitely slam me back into the rocks faster than I could reach for another hold.

Suddenly, God has a much more morbidly clever sense of irony than I had given Him credit for. Only moments before being taken, I had doubted it could possibly happen. Death by water seemed too much of a coincidence for a bad swimmer. That kind of drama was reserved for fictional protagonists. Now my wet, wet shoes tell me I had obviously underestimated life's love for an exciting climax.

I decide to call Tyson, my only resident contact in the small nearby beach town of San Juan Del Sur in southern Nicaragua. To my knowledge he did not have a boat, but with luck, he might just know someone who did. I wonder what to sound like as I dial. Should I try to keep my voice cool and calm to be as understandable as possible? Should I try to scream at the top of my lungs to be perfectly clear about how much danger I was in? It didn't matter either way. Just like I'd always read, cell phones could save lives, and it is about to do this for me, the cynical doubter who had never owned such a machine before this trip to Nicaragua as a freelance journalist.

But the irony continues. Punishing me for mocking them, the gods of wireless telecommunication refuse to grant me this call. Whatever Tyson is up to, he is not about to pick up his phone. I hang up and decide to try later. It is more important to start clambering away to the safety of the shore. Unfortunately, my cell has a different idea. It slips out of my hand and I watch, astonished, as it abandons itself to the foam and the blue. I briefly contemplate the idea of waiting to see if the waves would maybe return it. Then I realize they are just as likely to take me back so I make a run for it. My hands furiously slap the stones as I keep moving ever-right. The main town's shore, with its sandy beach, is just too far away, and who knows when the ocean would decide to have a go at me again? My arms already feel like soggy noodles.

I am horrified at the idea of dying like this, leaving a battered, unrecognizable corpse behind that none of the locals would care to really identify. My thoughts fly to my family, expecting me in a week. What will they say when my emails stop, when they try to reach me on my phone and, at best, some puzzled fisherman off the coast of Japan answers? I think of my friends next, the ones who had made it to my little going-away party and the ones who hadn't, particularly those I hadn't seen in ages. They go through their daily routines at work or at school, when suddenly they realize that they have not heard from me in a while. A phone call or an email later, they are mortified to learn that I have simply disappeared without a trace.

No, I will not die. I need to live. It just can't happen this way. My shoes are too heavy, soaking from my little dip earlier. I take them off. Now, clutching my shoes, I have only three free limbs in my quest for safety, and sharp, hot rocks are not exactly easy on the feet. I turn back to the water and throw the extra weight of the shoes away. The sea can take them along with the phone as long as the rest of me is intact.

NAVIGATING CUSTOMS

The footwear sinks momentarily, only to resurface, wiped clean of all dust and sand. Now gleaming a shiny black in the sun, my shoes float along ahead of me for a while, like a temptation to my increasingly blistery soles. I ignore them. It is not worth finding out if I can reach them without succumbing to the waves.

I am feeling sick and stupid for not paying more attention to the glaringly obvious full moon stuck in the sky the previous night, as clear a warning as could be about high tides. It was not too smart either, the idea of just walking along the cliff to clamber up and take pictures of the town, instead of heeding a local's suggestion to take a water-taxi to my destination point. However, I feel stupidest for coming down to Nicaragua as a freelance reporter in the first place, especially now that I could very likely die without even having published a single piece.

I arrive at a little inbound area of the shore, higher than the rest, where the waves just can't reach. A group of teenagers sits there, fishing. Their look as they see me is one of utter shock. I must be quite the sight: dripping from head to toe, tiny flesh wounds on my hands and feet, sticky hair, soaking pants and polo, and dirty, salt-covered glasses.

"Are you OK?" One of them asks.

"Yeah... I almost died but I'm fine now." They ask me if I need anything. I sit down next to them as they continue their fishing, probably still very confused. I cannot imagine what they think must have happened to me without hearing an explanation. I ask for water. One of them pours

Catching Waves

some into a bottle and gives it to me. As I empty it, the kids point at my various injuries in alarm. "It's nothing, really, it's nothing," I deadpan. After returning the bottle, I gaze at the coastline. There is still a final stretch to go before I reach the town.

As I thank the teenagers and start off, one of them catches up with me. "You don't have any sandals," he observes.

"Well, I had shoes but I had to throw them away," I reply, leaving the bewildered teen to turn to his friends. No doubt I would be the subject of some very interesting conversations that night. The story of the silly foreigner who did not take a boat to the cliff would become a part of the town lore by tomorrow.

The rest of the way seems easy. The waves have yet to recede, but the stones are a lot less massive. As I relax a little, realizing I would stay alive, the water shows me it has one more trick up its sleeve. The sheer force of the pounding tide begins to shake pebbles down from the top of the cliff at the shore. They rain down around me, hitting the stony coastline where I stand. I can't believe my luck at this point. As the pebbles get replaced by bigger and faster falling fist-sized rocks, I jump and run out of the way. I have left the territory of the dangerous and entered that of the absurd.

Finally, I make it to the beach. The hot sand bites at my feet but I do not care. I walk to one of the straw-roofed bars dotting the edges of the beach, and pick up two bottles of water. The cashier does not make a big deal about what I look like. Perhaps gringos who almost drown are not that uncommon around these parts after all.

Emptying one bottle on the spot, I take the other with me back to my budget hotel. I reach my room, making a point of avoiding anyone in the lobby, and collapse onto my bed, unable to fully understand what I have just been through. I think about my trip up to now, about all of the great stories that I would write and publish in major North American newspapers, and how they have all been rejected...

It is my fourth day in the country and I am nervously sitting across from Former President Jimmy Carter in a hotel lobby, hidden from the view of a local television crew's cameras as a reporter interviews him for his news program. Following the interview, I have been promised two questions with President Carter. I had been chasing him down since the day some strange coincidence put him and his crew on the same connecting flight as me from Atlanta. I am furiously jotting down notes as I try to decide which of my several questions I should choose.

His TV interview finally ends. The Nobel Peace Prize winner and highly respected former world leader turns to me with an expectant smile. There is a university backpack at my feet and my pen almost trembles in my fingers.

I ask him, "Will the unexpected death of presidential candidate Herty Lewites affect the upcoming elections?" Lewites, the most popular candidate in Nicaragua at the time, had tragically died of a heart attack just five days previous. "I don't think so," Mr. Carter says, explaining that he thinks Lewites' replacement should be able to pick up the pace.

"How have your own impressions of Nicaragua evolved from the time of your presidency until now?" I then ask him, echoing the clichéd "how do you feel?" I mentally repeat to myself that there are no stupid questions, hoping that this sacred mantra of journalism will become true through action.

He smiles fondly and tells me it's a very good question, so either my impromptu tactic has worked or he is simply too polite to acknowledge otherwise. I hastily record his reply, that he is happy the country's on the way to a real democracy and will hopefully continue to do so.

He then thanks the journalists and leaves.

My story is not published.

The sun beats down on me in the middle of a gigantic, exhilarated crowd, draped in red and black clothes and flags. I'm in the middle of putting my press pass back in my pocket, frustrated that a police officer would not let me into a cordoned-off area for the media where an elevated platform makes an ideal spot for taking pictures. It is Liberation Day, July 19, and 5,000 people are out to celebrate their freedom from the dictatorial Somoza regime. Unfortunately, as I feel the alarming amount of air in my pocket,

I realize that, at least for one reveller, an ideal celebration includes carefully lifting a turista's wallet.

Frustrated, I return to the police officer and complain. She tells me to go to the police and complain. "That's what I thought I was doing," I want to tell her, refusing to understand that I have to make my way to an actual station. I decide to give up. I had already removed any important documents from my wallet, which only contained five dollars anyway.

I send in my pictures to various newspapers. None of them get published.

Roberto Martinez sits across from me on a wooden stool in the middle of his tiny farm. His two small, sickly-looking dogs keep watch over his nearby chicken coop. Roberto is lamenting the unfairness of a newly signed free trade agreement with the United States. His family of five lives in two little shacks of two rooms each, with walls that do not rise all the way to the ceiling. Some apartments in Canada have bigger closets than any single one of his rooms. There is surprisingly little anger in Martinez's voice as he tells me he thinks the agreement, which sees the abolition of all trade tariffs between the U.S.A. and a number of Central American countries, will only benefit the rich: those big export farmers like in the coffee industry. He has no other source of income other than his farm, and fears he might be driven out soon.

Catching Waves

He describes a typical day in his life for me. He gets up at 5 am, when all is still dark and quiet, and goes to feed the fish in the small pond he owns. Then he has to feed his cattle, pack his corn into parcels, go to the market, check his crops, and help his wife with house chores. Martinez's day ends at around 11 pm, six hours before the next one starts. It is very hard to listen to him and not imagine that he will continue to do this for the rest of his working life.

Months and a veritable barrage of rejection emails later, this man's story is published, but the point is moot. There is no pride to be had in a few printed words and a byline next to the life of someone who will keep on toiling in dreadful living conditions.

Even if I didn't publish any of my stories, I at least would have one very wild tale of survival to tell for the rest of my life. In San Juan Del Sur, I get up and hit the shower at last. I am alive, and the blisters and sores on my feet will heal quickly enough. Furthermore, in a week I am returning to my family in Canada, where people do not work from 5 am to 11 pm, and do not live in apartments with walls that do not rise all the way to the ceiling. Every time that I complain from now on, about almost dying or about even more trivial annoyances, I will remember that somewhere a little further south, Roberto Martinez is probably working on his farm. He is exhausted because he has been up since 5 am, and he will do this again tomorrow, and the day after that, and the day after that one as well.

Stacey Bowman *is a novice traveller, a life-long writer and currently an editorial assistant at* Corporate Knights *magazine in Toronto. She will begin pursuing an MFA in Creative Writing at the University of Guelph-Humber in September, 2007.*

CLIMB TO THE SEA

IT IS MIDNIGHT ON our fifth full day in France. Camille's Renault hisses along the black pavement. Our heads, slick in moonlight, weave to the sound of our own voices. We're singing Beatles songs at the tops of our lungs.

Hey Jude, don't make it bad.
Take a sad song and make it better.

The Renault is smaller and colder than our parents' SUV's, but the songs are the same. We could be anywhere, yet beyond the car window the cold fields of Northern France stretch out from the seam of the road, a taut fabric of history, rough and pilled from years of war and resistance, but enduring still.

We've come to Lille by train from Paris, where we began our European tour. We're heavily bruised by excitement and fear. Our eyes still water—stuck by the needle of the Eiffel Tower as we lay on our backs beneath it. The scaffolding was covered by thousands of lights that twinkled and flashed like the CNE midway back home.

Melanie was mesmerized. Laura got a headache. I watched the groups of young people sprawled on blankets around us, the grass cropped to a green fuzz, littered with cigarette butts and bottle caps. I picked out their soft syllables without realizing, my ear drinking in the language.

In Paris the French is high and crisp—fast, but well enunciated. Like raindrops in a tin bucket. In Locon, a farming village of loosely scattered brick homes, flat browning pastures, cornfields and sloughs north of Lille, the accent is guttural and aged, even when it issues from the lips of Julien. He's Camille's best friend, a young human rights lawyer who drinks too much Affligem. He gives us a pronunciation lesson immediately: "Lo-con is a town. Le Con is a... well a disgusting word."

When Camille picks us up from the station, I immediately notice her overgrown body. She is knees and elbows all, with big feet and a beaked nose. Her eyes are too large and water colour blue. They study you, but are carefully guarded. I, usually unbowed by a direct stare, rarely look into them. We are careful around her.

Her mother is dead of cancer. A year since. Camille is the eldest of four. She has inherited her grandparents' farmhouse in Locon. It's 100 years old and smells of dirt and old curtains, emptied wine bottles, cattle manure and fireplace ashes. Hired help tends the cows, geese and cornfields, but the gardens are overgrown and the paint on the barn is peeling. Her three younger brothers still live at the family home in Frugge, a village of red brick and tiled roofs—the style of the north, Camille tells us—with her father, a farm-animal veterinarian and Sous Prefect for his municipality. We visit them for Sunday lunch, the biggest meal of the day.

The drive to Frugge is long and dusty, the road narrow, winding drastically through farming villages. The houses and clusters of stores inch up against the asphalt, leaning precariously over the road. The populations are largely stagnant. Families continue on for generations in the same village, the same plot of land. World War II is a living memory here. This is astonishing to us whose day-to-day lives are almost entirely free from any remembrance of those dark times. Young people here feel the presence of history in the very rooms they walk through each day. Farmhouses became resistance headquarters. Farmers and their wives processed fake documents between tending their weak crops and bony livestock. Camille's grandmother hid a Jewish couple in her hayloft.

Closer to the Belgian border, the devastation has been entirely erased. Dunkirk was so damaged it had to be rebuilt around what was left of its population. New walls encased old lives of impossible endurance. But inexplicably, the remains of concrete German bunkers still sit in farmers' fields from Ghent to Lille, growing dandelions on their grassy tops. No one is destroying them, preferring to let them molder and collapse under the slow march of time, cow after cow shitting in their doorways.

Camille's father's house is tucked into the main street corner of Frugge. It's part of a large stone building with a red tiled roof. The heavy wooden door is the width of two regular doors, outfitted with a brass doorknob too large for me to grasp with one hand. It takes both Melanie and me to push it shut behind us as we're ushered into the house by Camille's father, Jean-Marie. The rooms are filled with nineteenth-century furniture—blue velvet sofas, upholstered wooden chairs, an oval wall mirror framed in gold leaf. Sunlight streams in through the towering front window of the parlor where we're seated, hands folded in our laps. I look at the pictures of battles and old women hanging on the walls. Their clarity is compromised by a thick layer of dust.

The language barrier is more than we prepared for, but gradually Jean-Marie finds his English, and I overcome my fear of inadequacy and include French words in my polite inquiries. I hope he doesn't find my accent unpleasant. He is a robust, middle-aged man with friendly, tired eyes the same blue as Camille's. I like him immediately. The eldest brother, Remy, appears with flutes of champagne on a silver serving tray. This makes us shy, but it soon becomes clear that though we're being treated with deference, Jean-Marie likes to eat and drink well. He downs two glasses with an unaffected air as we sip self-consciously at ours. It is uncommonly good, and the general air begins to relax, though Camille pulls at her ponytail absently and pops crackers into her mouth in quick succession. I long for her to say something to ease the interaction. She doesn't, so I ask to see the garden.

Jean-Marie ushers me around the courtyard with evident pride. The walkway runs round a large square of grass where the two younger brothers, Louis and Henri,

Climb to the Sea

are juggling a soccer ball. The perpendicular beds are filled with carefully spaced rosebushes—orange teas and larger, thorny shrubs—interspersed with hydrangeas and, whimsically, small tomato plants. Jean-Marie's pride and joy are his pear trees. Three line each side of the square, meticulously pruned and bearing the last of the season's fruit. I examine the rough brown bodies closely, taking them gently in my palm. Jean-Marie is pleased. Camille and Remy's fiancé command the kitchen, but the garden is Jean-Marie's to nurture or destroy. I wonder if Camille's mother spent time there.

Melanie and Laura have found their way into the boys' game and I join them on the grass. Laughter makes up for the words we cannot say to one another. It's impossible to be unkind when the only effective means of communication is a smile. Camille appears on the patio.

"Girls! You play football?" She is standing motionless, hands on hips. She's astonished.

I wonder if she's being sarcastic. It's often hard to judge the connotation of her phrases because though her English is good, the cadence of her speech remains foreign. This is when I realize that Henri and Louis' laughter is incredulous, though very good-natured. They too, are surprised at our eager participation. All three are waiting for our explanation. Melanie looks slightly embarrassed.

"Yes," I say. "We play football. And hockey too."

The boys burst into laughter afresh. Perhaps they think I'm making a joke now, but the game goes on as before.

NAVIGATING CUSTOMS

Stacey Bowman

Lunch is a fresh spread of roast chicken with herbed potatoes, warm parmesan-crusted tomatoes and more champagne. The large mahogany table fits the nine of us comfortably. I am seated to the left of Jean-Marie, who commands the head fittingly. The other end of the table is empty. He eats fast in the matter of some middle-aged men—like it's their duty to keep up their appetite. I ask him about his prefecture and his work. He speaks with little animation about both, though his eyes are warm and seem to welcome the attention. Camille is chatting in rapid French with Remy's fiancé and the boys are shoveling the chicken as only teenagers can do. When their appetites are somewhat appeased, they begin to ask us questions about our schooling and where else we plan to go in Europe. Camille translates for Laura and Melanie. I try to answer in French. They're encouraging, but truly don't seem to understand most of what I attempt to say. Now there is much laughter, for we are all feeling a little inadequate. A silken custard tart is brought out for dessert. I hold each bite on my tongue, working the milky sweetness around my mouth. Jean-Marie excuses himself from the table, returning with five poached pears resting in a white china bowl.

"Please, try my pears, they are famous," he says. "They are my last ones."

The fruit is stained a rich maroon from the red wine, cloves and cinnamon in which it's been simmered. My fork sinks luxuriously into the grainy flesh. The taste is sweet at first, mellowing into a slightly bitter finish. The tannins from the wine dance pleasantly on my tongue.

Climb to the Sea

When I go to find the bathroom I notice how truly cavernous the house is. The ceilings are high as a church's, inspiring in me an absurd feeling of reverence, even while sitting on the toilet. I examine the molding around the ceiling, the vase of now dead roses beside the sink. Crinkled petals litter the basin. The voices of Camille and Remy waft up the air vent from the kitchen, disrupted by the clatter of plates. They're talking over one another in strained, clipped syllables. I don't understand their words but I feel the tension. The house seems permeated by a slow melancholia, a slight groaning of the baseboards—every step is an effort. For the first time since we left, I'm sad and homesick for my own family. I wonder if Camille comes here often. She lives nearly two hours away.

After lunch I climb into Julien's gray Peugeot and we wind through the countryside towards the coast. Camille and the other girls follow a distance behind. The rolling pastures give way to gentle forest as I chat in slow, deliberate English with Julien. He and Camille are both lawyers. They've been friends since law school, and both work in Lille. Julien represents immigrants trying to gain citizenship or avoid deportation. I ask him what he thinks of the new law preventing religious dress. He shakes his head.

"It is getting bad. There are many people in France who like having immigrants come to our country. But there are some who are scared of losing jobs. The immigrants are become—how to say it in English? Ghetto?"

"Ghetto-ized?" I offer.

"Yes. They do not find good jobs. I know some French will not give a immigrant a job over a French citizen. People are afraid of losing control."

I muse that it seems the whole western world is dealing with this problem. I tell him it is splitting Canadians, too. We are proud of our inclusive attitude, but Toronto is full of cabbies who hold PhDs from their home countries.

"It is the same here. And in the North, you look around, there are not many immigrants. Here people like things to stay always like they are," Julien says.

He worries about what will happen with racial tensions rising and right-wing political parties growing stronger. He himself votes communist, though he points out he doesn't agree with everything they stand for, either.

"Something will happen soon, I think. There is tension. There is anger."

I watch his face as he talks of the man he tried to save from deportation to Pakistan. It becomes hard, loses its boyishness.

Our car pulls into the tiny town of Montreuil Sur Mer, a beautiful, mediaeval village miraculously untouched by the wars. It is built on a high embankment, anchored by the ruins of a citadel. We clamber over what's left of the ramparts. Through holes in the crumbling walls, we take in views of the countryside, framed by the arching arms of ancient trees. A blue finger of sea rests on the horizon—a thin slip of water separating France from England.

Climb to the Sea

Cobbled roads lead us through the town's centre, where gift-shops and cafés cater to tourists. Tumbles of colourful flowers cascade over rock walls along the streets and spill out of baskets and window boxes on every building. This is the village that inspired Victor Hugo's *Les Misérables*, Camille tells us. I have not bothered to find out whether this is indeed true. Regardless of fact, I have now pictured each scene of the novel in the streets of this beautiful town, and I have no wish to alter these visions.

Le Touquet, a resort town on the ocean, is the day's final stop. It's a smaller version of Ocean City, complete with all the party sensibility. The streets of pubs and bars and clusters of gray-sided condos give it away, though when we arrive the town is virtually empty. The beach is a huge expanse of flat sand and tide pools, the ocean undulating at its edge, reflecting the late afternoon sky. It is a calm palette of blue, gray and white, screened by thin clouds now and again. We park the car and take off our shoes in order to climb the sand dunes and hillocks that separate the road from the beach. The wind is aggressive but warm, and we roll up the cuffs of our jeans and cast our sweaters on the long grass that pokes through the dunes.

"Let's run!" says Camille, and she heads off towards the water without pausing to see if we are following, her long legs pumping gracefully and tangled hair whipping wildly behind her. I shrug and begin to run after her, leaving the other three to laugh at us. I run regularly at home, but have not engaged in any physical effort since beginning our trip. The increased flow of blood in my legs is welcome. As my breathing quickens, I begin to feel a tremendous rush of adrenalin and I can't help but smile as I fully appreciate where we are—the edge of France. England is across from us, Belgium to the right, Normandy to the left, and the sky a huge expanse of light—endless and inviting. I'm glad we're alone on the beach. It's fall and too chilly for the summer crowds. This is all ours, the day is ours, the sea and the sand and the sky. All thoughts of my life at home, worries, problems and uncertainties drop away from my body as I charge along the sand, splashing through tide puddles and breathing the salty air. Coming out of my reverie, I see Camille has reached the water. I slow to a walk and watch her silhouette against the horizon. She is standing with her legs slightly apart, her hands open and hanging heavily by her sides. She looks out, unmoving.

"Work is not life."

This is Camille's answer to my innocent inquiry into whether or not she enjoys her job at her law firm. We are sitting cross-legged on the beach, careless of the sand creeping beneath our waistbands and up our pant legs.

"Work is not life. I need more time," she repeats. I examine the fine pale sand.

"It is my friends and my family that are life. I like my job, but sometimes it is too busy. It's not important, to be so busy."

Climb to the Sea

I understand these statements completely—or at least I think I do. Losing someone must make you eager for life in some ways, and make you dread it in others.

Julien, Laura and Melanie have reached us now, and we get up and pose for pictures. A fisherman in yellow hip-waders fiddles with his nets on the sand a short distance away. Camille runs over and speaks with him in French. She beckons to us.

"He will be in a picture with you," she says excitedly.

We pose awkwardly around him. I don't want him to think we're shallow tourists, peering at the locals like they're museum exhibits, but he is smiling warmly as the beeps of our digital cameras go off one after the other.

Julien takes more pictures of us as we horse around in the water and draw our names in the sand with our toes. We run and laugh and turn our faces to the sinking September sun. And then we walk in a line towards the car, our feet leaving gentle imprints in the sand.

The long drive back to Locon is quiet and dark. I look at Camille beside me in the driver's seat—her back is straining towards the wheel, her neck slightly bowed. She is silent, but looks content enough, though her long fingers grip the wheel with unnecessary force. I was hoping to know her more after this weekend than I do. I don't really know her at all, I think to myself, despite being admitted into her world. I wonder if this is how it will be everywhere—a quick skim over the surface of a place, fleeting moments of depth, but not enough to piece together a truth. The history in Europe runs deep. It is buried in the soil, scratched into the walls, dissolved like sediment in the very water. The people are the same. History courses through their veins—their own, their family's. Why would they bleed for us, mere strangers who've come to learn and appreciate something we cannot fully understand?

In the twilight the bunkers are still visible, like the backs of sleeping animals. Camille says the red roofs of the North aren't simply the style anymore. They're the law. Every new building must have one to preserve uniformity and identity. But esthetics are only that, I think, and who will preserve what lies beneath? Should it be preserved? "There is tension," Julien said. Between the red roofs and the lives lived beneath them. Between who people are and who they appear to be. And we, accepting and open as we are, can perceive only this surface.

Singing was Camille's idea. French or Canadian, everyone knows the Beatles. She's barely able to hold on to consciousness after driving us across these miles of countryside. "Let it Be" escapes from the open windows of the Renault as we pull into Camille's drive. The geese honk, flap about and scatter. The cows shift in their stalls, their weight causing the wood to creak and groan. Camille unfolds her long, skinny body from the driver's seat. She appears almost skeletal in the stark headlights. The air is chill and damp, and crickets compete with our hearty strains.

Whisper words of wisdom
Let it be.

Camille sings and sings as we climb the wooden stairs, her voice undiminished within the thin walls of the old house. I walk to the window in our bedroom and push aside the curtain. A smoky mist lies over the fields like a blanket. The moon is shrouded in cloud. Its muted glow casts just enough light to illuminate the slick line of road at the edge of the pasture. I am looking north, towards the sea.

Weeks later we will watch CNN coverage of the Paris riots from our hostel bar in Germany. We will receive worried emails from Camille and Julien asking where we are and warning us against returning to France anytime soon. We'll be surprised and touched they are thinking of us. There will be pictures sent, too. Of us running on the beach, against the backdrop of ocean and sky. They will look familiar, but somehow more beautiful than we remember. At the bottom, a simple caption: From Julien.

christine estima *is a playwright, novelist, actress, and arts journalist sleeping in some forgotten corner of a European railway station. Her writing has appeared in* The Malahat Review, The Encyclopedia of Modern Drama, Matrix Magazine, TheGate.ca, NOW Magazine, *and will soon be seen in* Room of One's Own *and* Canadian Theatre Review. *Her short story "Nylon-Encased Flesh" was included in the literary anthology* ToK: Writing the New Toronto *(2006). Playwrighting credits include,* Vignettes In The Dark *(2004, Toronto Fringe Festival) and* The Spadina Monologues *(2005, The New Ideas Festival, Alumnae Theatre; Theatre Passe Muraille backspace). christine holds an MA in Interdisciplinary Studies from York University. Having traveled across the Middle East, Europe, christine is now living in the UK, but you'll still find her, most likely, in the fridge at 4 am.*

BETWEEN BERLIN AND BEIRUT

SEPTEMBER 2005

BEIRUT, LEBANON

The day is an ultrablue. The city swelters. Arabic prayer chants wail through the narrow streets of distorted cobblestones and asphalt in the Hamra district of Beirut. Neighbouring gelato cafés amplify the American Top 40 radio station. Palm trees necklace the curves of La Corniche: a long stretch of boardwalk, sand, and cliffs along the Mediterranean coast. The gilt streets tentacle from Place D'Étoile, the heart of downtown Beirut stores, sporting haute couture for the nouveau-riche in display windows. Family-owned fruit markets sell football-sized pomegranates for only 1000 Lebanese Lira each. Old men with argyle caps carry baskets of loose grain and husks on their backs. Large terra-cotta jars brandish freshly sprouting herbs. The rabid sun slices through yellow stucco buildings shrouded with magenta bougainvillea, between cedar trees and multiplexes, sentries in sentry boxes, and parakeets in flamboyant bushes.

Prayers echo. Allah o akbar. La allah illa allah. Leering men, cigarette smoke, magazine vendors, pigeons dancing, office towers. Maronites. Druze. Orthodox. Sunni. Shoe shiners on their knees, strays cats pawing Styrofoam, jeweled Narghiles in shop windows. Saudi Arabian cloaks sold next to Armani suits. Majestic city postcards: Byblos, Rachaya, Tyre, Baalbeck, Jounieh, Chekka.

Walking through the congested city, the 40°C heat is debilitating. The travel guidebook to Lebanon says that I should dress modestly and at least wear pants. In the ferocity of the Middle Eastern climate, all around me are jeans and long slacks. Christian women wear tank tops and tight-fitted clothing, but I've yet to see an exposed calf or thigh. Muslim women walk completely covered in black Abbayas with intricate embroidery, but the hems stop short of their ankles to reveal their sexy open-toed stilettos, high enough to rival Paris Hilton's. When I reach the Al Sa'a Café in the heart of Place D'Étoile, the waiters stare at my bare legs as they adjust the seating arrangements of the outdoor patio.

I order all the dishes that my Sitto—my grandmother—makes me back home in Montréal. As the plates arrive I immediately shove three fingers of garlic humus into my mouth. Nibble on a handful of chewy black olives. Finish off the teardrop-shaped vegetarian kibbeh. Kousa, hollowed baby vegetable marrow, pregnant with rice and minced meat stewed in tomatoes. And a falafel sandwich, fried with sesame seeds, and wrapped in warm Syrian bread with pickled red beets, parsley, and mint leaves.

Between Berlin and Beirut

Cars zoom in disorientation and complete chaos. The traffic lights don't work, and are hardly obeyed when they do work. Vespas zoom into oncoming traffic.

Soldiers stand in camouflage in front of gilt palaces and 12th century mosques, gripping their AK 47s to their thighs. People throw their empties on ancient Gallo-Roman columns that are barely standing. Photos and banners of assassinated Prime Minister Rafik Hariri adorn every window. The soaring iron monument erected in Martyrs' Square in tribute to revolutionary heroes is, ironically, bullet-ridden. The Holiday Inn, which was erected before the civil war, still stands with so many ammunition rounds speckling its surface, I wonder if it's structurally sound. The snipers sabotaged it. No windows, no paint, only concrete, rubble, and millions of tiny exit wounds. It stands completely hollowed behind the Intercontinental Phoenician. I stare at it long enough to begin to feel the war zone effect.

Penetrated. Punctured. Wounded. Disaster upon disaster. Wreckage upon wreckage.

But the Mediterranean water is so enviably blue. I amble along La Corniche in the scorch of the day and pause in front of the Pigeon Rocks to ponder. The only natural feature of Beirut, the Pigeon Rocks are twin Limestone formations that the sea undulates between, like the Percé Rock in Gaspé, Quebec.

One hundred and five years ago, my great-grandmother sailed away from these shores to find herself. One hundred

NAVIGATING CUSTOMS

and five years later, her great-granddaughter returns to these shores for the same reason.

As night falls, I return to the now packed Place D'Étoile, watching the men in Turkish hats display their gilt narghile sets. In the square, a man kicks around a huge beach ball with his toddler son, his daughter hoisted upon his shoulders. Another little boy blows bubbles that rise lightly through the azure sky. Two little girls in pig-tails zoom in circles on their pink training-wheeled bicycles. Families laugh as they slurp up sugarplum and mango ice cream. Photographers perfectly time the lavish entrance of a bride sitting up on the back seat of a convertible, waving to the prestigious guests like a pageant queen in a parade, into the St. George's Orthodox Cathedral in the square. Downtown Beirut has returned to its glorious "Paris of the East." Nothing I have been told about the Middle East is true. Those are remnants of a bad dream.

I think about the 15 years of war that ravaged this city. How the streets ran red and the city crumbled. When peace finally came, I can only imagine the relief that these people collectively heaved in their sighs as they swept the rubble from their ankles and let their children open their eyes. The monsters died under the bed.

July 2006

Berlin, Germany

Sitting in the basement kitchen of my hostel, I've flipped on the TV, already set to CNN, the only English channel. I am piecing together from random video clips and images splashed across the screen what has happened in Beirut. Hezbollah. Israel. Abductions. Human shields. Retaliations. Destruction. Wreckage. Carnage. I see glimpses of areas I had walked through. Faces I'm sure I know. A spattering of rubble across a street that I had run through like a riot.

The television won't let go of me. It shows the sun breaking through dust clouds. Explosions raise the sand all night. Almost a year later, I've been to so many cities and locations, but Beirut haunts me across the planet. That old boar has claws that dig into my skin. The distance between Berlin and Beirut is only a couple thousand kilometers, and it's shrinking. I want to set fire to the television. To CNN. Perhaps only then would it be possible to get away. To cauterize.

The camera zooms in on chaos, towers blown apart like leaves in centrifugal gusts, mothers wearing hijabs cradling children in Levi jeans. Shelters. Hospitals. In the distance, beyond Mount Lebanon, the calm azure of the Mediterranean. Where is the Beirut I know? Where are the streets my great-grandmother traversed?

I dash out into the calm streets of Berlin, a former war zone turned cosmopolitan metropolis, and find myself facing the last remnants of the Berlin wall. I look up and down the protected relic. Spray paint from 1989 still vibrant with meaning. "MADNESS" someone had scrawled across the concrete slabs. That's what East Berliners said the passage to the West felt like. When the walls fell and all Berliners were able to shake hands with each other. But my passage from East to West is a madness without triumph. The madness will be continuous, and like a python, it swallows me whole.

Amy Klassen *grew up in various cities within British Columbia, Canada. During the summer after her high-school graduation she volunteered in Guyana, South America, with Youth Challenge International. Amy now attends Carleton University in Ottawa, Ontario, double majoring in English and Human Rights.*

White Girl Goes Deaf in Guyana

"NO MEANS NO, BUT if you say no you better believe I will beg, and beg, and beg. And once I begged so hard I cried." My neck arched away from the wooden floor as I laughed, tears rolling out of the corners of my eyes and into my ears. We, an unlikely group gathered from Canada, Guyana, and Ireland, were lounging inside a skeleton of boards suspended on four stilts, discussing the intricate attitudes of our respective cultures toward sex. Poster boards and survey papers were strewn around, as limp from the humidity as we were.

"And if you're dancing in a club, and if you don't get a, you know, hard-on, in like the first two songs, she will be so insulted she'll walk away, you be lucky if she don't, she doesn't, slap you." Leroy was from Georgetown, Guyana's capital. He and Erin were our group leaders. They had led us into the jungle for days, on the backs of trucks, on ferries, trekking through villages, and finally twisting down Pomeroon River on two small motorboats to get to Liberty, our first destination. Our assignment was to educate. First ourselves, about the people and dynamics of the villages we were to inhabit, and then the locals, about basic health and sex education, but mainly the people heading our volunteer organization, about everything we gleaned from the people about themselves and their towns' needs. So far, the only one attempting any kind of education was Leroy, and he had his hands full trying to force our culture-shocked little brains behind another people's eyes. Even his experiences were far different from those of the people who stared into the clearing around the schoolhouse and then vanished as soon as we said "hi." Leroy had been to university in the crowded, Americanized capital, where there were things like dance clubs and condoms... and health clinics. I sat up, careful not to get splinters in my palms, and noted a dark smudge on the edge of our world. Dusk would soon tumble in with a surge of mosquito wings and proboscis, and it was time for our last drenching of the day in an effort to cool our bodies enough for sleep. It was also time to challenge myself to another game of Chicken. While my group members stuck close to the riverbank, one hand firmly on the prow of our boat while scrubbing discreetly with the other hand beneath the opaque brown water, I dove off the back end of the boat and swam out into the water until horror stories of piranhas made me gasp and splash like a madwoman toward the dock. I usually lasted about thirty seconds. Then we dashed for our hammocks, mosquitoes and flies merrily clogging our throats and noses, and dove under our nets, tying the edges securely beneath us. We stayed there from 6:30 in the evening till dawn, entertained by Lariam-infused dreams, or the conversations between other sleepers who were having Lariam-infused dreams.

Days passed, with people sometimes appearing in our little fort only to dash away when they were noticed.

White Girl Goes Deaf in Guyana

You know you're doing a bad job of integrating into a village when you can't even find the villagers. Every hour or so I would dive off the boat and bob with the floating coconuts.

Eventually, I lost my game of Chicken, but not to a piranha. Someone should have told me that flowing mud is dirty, though I should have guessed that something was off when I saw a school of four-eyed fish skipping across the water and trying madly to swim onto land. My troubles started with an irritating earache in my left ear. The next day it was half plugged, and my right ear was starting to hurt. The day after that, I woke up completely deaf, and couldn't open my jaw more than a centimeter. It felt as though someone was repeatedly stabbing me, in through my ears and out my forehead. I swallowed our group's cache of amoxicillin within the next four days, but things just got worse. I couldn't sleep because of the pain, and even once (or twice) started crying because I couldn't handle it.

And then Erin started peeing blood.

Group consensus was that we would go to the closest hospital, which was in a town called Charity, first thing the next day. At that point I couldn't swallow, either, so I hadn't eaten for at least twenty-four hours when we left at five the next morning. Erin and I discovered that our boats were stuck firmly in the muck but, fortunately, we hadn't planned to use one of ours anyway: even with our most powerful motorboat it would have taken us at least six hours to get to Charity. It made much more sense to hitch-hike.

The wealthier families along the Pomeroon invested in small speedboats, and ran a kind of taxi service up and down the current. To "hail" one we simply had to jump up and down, shout, and wave our arms. The first boat of the morning ignored us, but when the next one went by an hour and a half later we made such a ridiculous display that the drivers must have taken pity on us. Or, more likely, assumed we had no idea what the going rate was, or what our money was worth. After some yelling the boaters realized that, despite her blonde hair, Erin was completely familiar with Guyanese currency, but they welcomed us onto their boat anyway.

As we sped along, I was amazed to see how many people were out on their boats and, instead of the ragged muddy shorts or T-shirts I usually saw them clothed in, were dressed in tuxedos and full lacy dresses buttoned up at collars and wrists. Whole families were piled into rickety wooden canoes, paddling away, but at the same time looking serenely ahead with backs straight and ties tied. I suddenly realized it was Sunday; they all must be going to church.

Two hours later, we dragged ourselves off the boat-taxi and plodded uphill on a dirt road toward the hospital. That took another hour, probably because we were basically crawling at this point. Erin was trying so hard not to pee that tears squeezed out from her lower lids; she really wanted to postpone the pain as long as possible.

White Girl Goes Deaf in Guyana

Charity Hospital looked empty except for a group of four or five nurses playing cards around a table. They didn't look up as Erin spoke to them. I couldn't hear a thing, but the emptiness of the hospital and the lack of enthusiasm exuding from the nurses started to worry me. With shouts and gestures, Erin helped me piece together the fruitless conference.

"Can we see a doctor?" asked Erin.

"No."

Disbelief. "No doctor?"

"No."

"Is the doctor out?"

"Yes."

"For how long?"

"Two days. So is the medic."

"Well, can we use your phone?"

"No."

Even Erin was at a momentary loss. The next town with a hospital was Sudbury, but what if we got there and found ourselves in another empty hospital? As soon as we stepped outside, all the rain that had failed to come down to float our boats in the morning broke through the sky in a waterfall. Erin took out her small umbrella and we huddled together to steady ourselves. The rain, however, couldn't have cared less about the umbrella and simply went around it. The trenches on either side of the road instantly filled with torrents of mud, so we got onto the road before we were swept away.

An interesting fact about Guyana is that the drivers there do not use brakes. They use horns instead. I, however, could not hear their warnings, so when Erin heard a noise behind us she had to shove me over into the muddy trench. This is how we straggled back down to the river's edge, where we went into a little store we had stopped at on our first journey into the jungle. We had befriended the amazingly generous and bubbly owner, whose name was Juice Man. Among other things, he sold plastic baggies of extraordinary cherry juice. At his store he offered us his phone book and phone to call the Sudbury Hospital. While Erin made sure a doctor was there, Juice Man hailed us a car-taxi. We had no energy left for shouting matches; we just paid the outrageous price, at least five times the usual, and leaned into the backseat.

An hour later we were sitting on the floor of a crowded waiting room. I dropped off to sleep but a nurse shook my shoulder, saying something. I stood up, confused and unhearing. She asked me a question, walked away, came back and pulled me along with her into a hall. She got the attention of two other nurses, who also started to talk at me. We were all very frustrated. Erin was down the hall ahead of me, talking to someone else. She yelled to my nurses when she saw us trying vainly to communicate, then came over to explain things to them. I was put in a room, where the doctor tried to talk to me too; I had to keep

White Girl Goes Deaf in Guyana

gesturing to a nurse to remind him that I couldn't hear. They pushed and pulled me where they wanted me to go, then the doctor poked instruments into my ears while I tried not to scream. He was as surly as all doctors should be, then wrote out a prescription and told me to take aspirin for the pain.

Erin was waiting in the hall for me, with the same prescription in her hand. I wondered why we didn't go directly to a pharmacy, but it turned out that we had a cache of that medication already back at camp. After we backtracked "home" to Liberty, Erin looked the medication up in her drug guide, which warned very emphatically against taking aspirin with it. I started to realize why she was our leader.

Later, when I had regained some hearing, Erin told me what the nurses had been so anxious to ask: "They wanted to know if you were white!" I was delighted. Apparently the muddy Pomeroon had permeated not just my ears, but my skin and my soul, too.

NAVIGATING CUSTOMS

Sarah-Jean Krahn *is currently finishing a Bachelor's degree in Honours English at the University of Calgary. Next year, she will be heading to McMaster to do a Master's in Cultural Studies and Critical Theory. She hopes to continue pursuing revisions to postcolonial theory and expansions to the definition of a text. Creative non-fiction is one awesome arena for these things to be done. She thanks to Clara Joseph for helping her get this far. [Splendid]...[!]"*

A Very Special Place

NO ONE IS HERE at first, but after I blink, people materialize out of nowhere, a swarm where there first was only me and Eric. These people buzz. They have furrowed brows, but mostly they gawk. I stand on my tiptoes to see over the cement blocks. I must gawk, too.

But there's not much to gawk at. It's nothing but a construction site. What have I been expecting? Maybe the twin beams of light I have read about. How ethereal. You could reach out to them but they would evade you. Or a pile of rubble and ashes. Fossilized, so everyone would always remember, and lament. Or furrow the brow, cluck the tongue, then gawk. How else can you mourn in the middle of a buzzing city as wide and intimidating as New York?

It's not that no one cares. I can feel it in the air. These people wouldn't be here if they didn't care. But they don't really know what to make of it all. Their expressions are ambiguous. Their voices are low. They point, and talk to their companions without looking into each other's eyes.

Sarah-Jean Krahn

Admittedly, I'm a little out of it. I don't know why I'm here. I told my mom that if I came here I would say a prayer for the lives lost and the families of the deceased, etc. Her request came around the same time I was reading for the first time about the Haditha massacre in Iraq, where some marines went crazy after the death of their comrade – can you call it a comrade, or is that too Soviet? – and murdered a bunch of people in their homes, including women and children; the usual product of war when everyone's sour after the first 48 hours. And then I read the next day that a little girl who had watched the brutal killing of her family was calling for the execution of the marines responsible. Oculus oculo. I thought, the world is in a mess. A very astute observation on my part. But I knew that if I came here, I wouldn't just be praying for the people my mom was thinking of. I would be imploring the ground and the air around me for peace in all people's hearts.

But is that why I came? I'm not sure. When we woke up this morning, Eric asked me what I wanted to do today. We had toyed with various ideas of what to do on our last day together; go down the shore, come into the city. I said I'd be okay with either, but if we came into New York, the only thing I really cared to see right now was the World Trade Center site. I called it Ground Zero when we talked. It was strange for me to talk that way, because I've wanted to visit New York City for so long. My friend Neesha and I spent years working on a series of Friends fanfics called Queen of Hearts, and since it took place in New York it was a meaningful place for me and my past. So why did I only want to see this place, this anti-place, this emptiness, when there was so much more for me to take in? When I

A Very Special Place

got out of the shower that morning, Eric informed me that he had called to find out about the bus schedule and we were going into the city to do what I really wanted to do. Or was it what he really wanted to do?

I see a sign. "Please help us to maintain this site as a very special place. Please do not purchase any items or services here, or donate money to people soliciting here, so that this place can be fully appreciated by all visitors. THE PORT AUTHORITY OF NY & NJ"

This is a very special place.

Someone is showing Eric a thin flipbook of digital images of rubble and ashes, twin beams of light. So here's what I expected to see. Eric taps his index finger against a picture. "Look." I see flames and thick smoke. I can't register what the picture is of, because the smoke is in my eyes, and Eric thrusts the flipbook back at the person. "No thanks," he says. To me, "I have all those pictures at home, anyway."

The person is swallowed into the crowd before I can even really see him. I'm thinking of national parks, where uniformed rangers and interpreters are paid to teach and guide tourists. I kind of thought maybe that was why this person with the flipbook was here. But I guess he was trying to sell it to us.

"Look." I poke Eric's upper arm repeatedly, and point to the sign. This is a very special place. "They don't want you buying stuff here, anyway. They think it's disrespectful." I think the sign is funny. I don't think I know how

NAVIGATING CUSTOMS

to fully appreciate this very special place whether or not people purchase, donate, and solicit around me. Still, when I show him, I'm serious, mainly because I know it's important to Eric to be as respectful as possible.

I'm right. He only glances at the sign, then moves away from me. His voice is angry when he speaks. "You don't have to show me about respect when it comes to this place."

There's a steel fence around the construction site, which collapses a few stories into the ground. They must be building a basement. Eric stands at the fence. I go to stand beside him, anxious. "I wasn't criticizing," I explain. "I just wanted to show you."

Eric's over it pretty quickly. He ignores me at least. He's snapping pictures on his cell phone. I wonder what he's taking pictures of. He says, "It wasn't just the World Trade Center that was destroyed. There were at least twelve buildings that were affected." I think, there were at least twelve people that were affected. There were at least twelve states that were affected. There were at least twelve countries that were affected.

I dwell on Eric's previous abruptness of attitude, and start taking some pictures to distract myself. There's a pedestrian sign. And a cross appearing to be "naturally" formed by remnants of steel beams. I wonder when the pedestrian sign came into the picture, and who could walk there, behind the fence. I think in New Jersey pedestrians have the right of way like in Canada, but the law is pretty much ignored. Does New York have a similar law?

A Very Special Place

"I'm sure you've seen that picture on the news many times," Eric says, referring to the cross. I haven't. Either I didn't watch enough news or good old defamiliarization failed me as I flipped from channel to channel. "For two months there was no normal TV here," he continues. I think he's exaggerating, but how would I know? This is not my home.

Do I think that because I'm from Canada, I'm not complicit with the world's injustices? Am I isolated from everything I see here? Does the fence keep me out of the loop of violence? My thoughts are random and transfix me as I stare through a square in the fence. I notice Eric back away but I do not turn away. Is this it? Are we done already? I'm not ready to leave.

"Come on," he says, and I reluctantly go over to him. Eric takes me by the wrist and we pace the sidewalk along the fence to a road filled with pedestrians. It reminds me vaguely of Stephen Avenue, because there is an orange and black roadblock indicating that traffic is not welcome, but then again, Stephen Avenue doesn't normally have police cars parked half on the sidewalk, red and blue lights flashing. A policewoman seems to be securing the area, keeping watch over the roadblock. Actually, more than a quaint outdoor shopping area for pedestrians, the blockade makes the street look like it's being quarantined for a parade. Pedestrians mill in the street behind the roadblock as taxis whiz by in the perpendicular lanes. More vehicles are parked along the street, white trucks. "No Parking Except FDNY." I think, that police car shouldn't be there.

Sarah-Jean Krahn

I guess the Fire Department is friends with the Police Department.

The Fire Department is a light-grey building, antique in its rounded mouldings. As we reach the corner of the building, I see a tiny window at eye level with the curtain drawn. A picture, drawn in crayon by a child's hand, is taped to the glass. The purple and yellow people in the drawing are holding hands. "Thank you FDNY" in a determined scrawl. Gratitude is so easy, so innocent, in the kinder years.

We turn the corner of the fire hall, and a copper cast spans the width of the wall. It shows the twin towers, having been hit by airplanes, exploding with copper dust, billowing with copper smoke. Firefighters with their trucks and hoses. A tugboat on the water in the background. Other buildings, shorter in stature than the ones burning, look on, like curious bystanders at the scene of an accident. "MAY WE NEVER FORGET." A girl is getting her picture taken beside the cast of the towers. She is grinning. Since her photographer is on the far side of the sidewalk, Eric and I wait for the flash before walking by. The girl skips over to her companion to see the thumbnail of herself on the digital camera.

Under the remainder of the cast, a list of names dominates. I do not recognize any names. Does everyone scan such lists and try to find a personal connection? Like in *Gone With the Wind*, when the soldier comes into Atlanta with the official list of dead, and mothers crumple to the ground when they hear their sons' names recited.

A Very Special Place

"This is a list of all the firefighters from here who helped. But departments came over from Jersey, even. From my town, from Heights, even." Many of the names are accompanied by strange symbols: stars, rectangles, circular badges. Eric gestures to the rectangular symbol and says, "This means the person died in the World Trade Centre... maybe. I think it does." But at the end of the list there is a legend and we realize all the names are names of firefighters, and the symbols indicate their rank. "Oh, I guess not," he amends with a mumble. He turns away and starts to walk back toward the fence of the site. I think he is tense about his mistake, like he is automatically supposed to know everything about this place. I sigh, and follow, walking backwards as I take a few shots of my own. No person is in the picture I take of the towers.

Back at the chain-link fence, Eric holds the links with his middle and index fingers, and stares stonily at an altar ten metres behind.

> "Thank You America
> For Your Prayers and Support For
> All Those Lost And Their Families
> From The Port Authority NY & NJ Police"

The altar is neatly pasted with badges and medallions, and topped with hats, toy trucks, birdhouses, picture frames, and a generous arrangement of lilies and roses. "I got to go in there when I was in uniform to pay my respects," Eric murmurs thoughtfully. "It looked a lot different before. More cluttered. More personal." Eric is quiet for a moment—reliving the experience? I notice that now the altar is kept neat and symmetrical, probably with only a fraction of the offerings. Where are the others?

When Eric speaks again, his voice is normal. "Rico and I came for a vigil and Rico was kind of like—why don't I get to go in?" He chuckles. I don't say anything. I think it's ironically sad that the very people being thanked by the sign on the altar are not allowed to approach the altar. "Thank You America." Is Rico less American than Eric? And why isn't that one "and" capitalized, while the other is? I shake my head clear and purse my lips. Security reasons, I suppose.

Why am I here? Now, even in the day's bright sunshine, I can see Eric breaking. That voice was just a cover. We're not touching, but I feel that his heart must be beating fast, and he's looking down, around, anywhere but that altar or my eyes. He's lightly stamping his feet, like a young fawn unsure of where to lay his hooves; the next place he steps could be a gopher hole. His hand now covers his face, his eyes; his upper back is heaving lightly. Crying. I must be here for a reason. I must be here to comfort Eric, to give him hope.

I don't hesitate in putting my arms around his shoulders, his neck. If he can't see me through the tears, he must know that I'm here through my touch. But he shrugs me away. "Get off of me." His act is aggressive, his words harsh. They sting so much. The tears sting in the corners of my eyes, too. WHY am I here?

A Very Special Place

Even when Eric sucks in his breath and glances at me sideways, even when he says, "Just hold my hand," I know there is no going back. No matter why I came here, I'm broken now.

NAVIGATING CUSTOMS

Alex Leslie has worked as a journalist, including a stint as National Features Bureau Chief for Canadian University Press. She will begin her MFA in Creative Writing at UBC in the fall, focusing on short fiction. Her travels have taken her to Spain and Morocco, all over coastal BC, and recently to St. Petersburg, Russia, to participate in writing workshops with the Summer Literary Seminars program.

Bulls Coursed Through
My Dreams All Night

"You are either very brave or very stupid."

This the man told me as I stood waiting to board a bus deeper into the Spanish Pyrenees. I had just told him that I was travelling alone—a white, 21-year-old Canadian woman in remote northern Spain. Just come from Barcelona where the plane had landed me, curving up into the Pyrenees then down to Pamplona, Madrid, then farther South, falling towards the blue band that separates Europe from Africa. That was my route, a vague line that I had drawn across my small creased map, each inkblot spanning miles that meant days. This was the third month of a slow summer after a devastating year. My planned career path had sunk and shifted under ruptured friendships, abandoned schoolwork, a job I could not go back to. Next year, I told myself, I would return to university, devote myself to books. Before then the rubble needed to be reconfigured, a landscape dug out of the cracked bedrock of the past months, the shattered directions somehow realigned.

I bought my ticket on a Friday, left that Monday. A Monday in late June, Vancouver vanishing past the aeroplane's windows in a series of blue flashes: bright welts left on water by a skipping stone. My departure was urgent, but I left with detachment. Somehow I had chosen Spain, its heat and colour and trashing dance, because I wanted the trip burnt into me.

"I guess I'm both."

I looked at the man. His nose had been broken earlier in life, regrown like a thorn out of his face. Jutting elbows and knees, his head carved from one piece of walnut. A graceful, demented mountain puppet.

"Watch yourself."

"I am."

"This country is different from Canada."

I had received other warnings before this. In Barcelona a waiter at an outdoor patio demonstrated how a thief would reach under my chair from behind. You see? You see? Now you have no backpack! He spidered around me in his tuxedo, holding his prize high above his head. The woman at the tourist centre suggested I purchase a small knife, carry it in a safety sheath with my money and passport.

"I've travelled before."

And I meant it, then.

"Where?"

Bulls Coursed Through My Dreams All Night

"France, England and Scotland. My older sister lives near San Francisco."

He didn't respond. Turned away, laughing.

The bus arrived. A bus used only by locals, the last public transport before the border with France. Heading up to the tiny border villages, outposts in the mountains gathered around cobble-fisted churches.

"You don't want Spain."

He said this, thinking I couldn't hear, as the bus stilled hackingly.

Two linked valleys high in the Pyrenees, four villages strung along one stone road like beads on a necklace. For a few dollars a night I slept in the loft of the administrative building of a campground. In the morning I walked into the nearest village to eat.

One pub. I found a stool and ordered by pointing at the tapas set out on plates on the counter. Cold omelette, a plate of gritty black sausage, bread, a mug of beer that tasted like honeyed lead. My guidebook contained only a shrunken map of the area, valleys drawn in hair-lines like organs on a biological chart from the eighteenth century. Spanish was not spoken here, nor French. My ersatz translational skills didn't work. Here, Castilian: their own dialect. A muscular blend of the language that had occupied and moved through. Existence on the borderline made the space difficult to navigate, soaked in words made just for these four villages, this one road. Their language had emerged from the spaces forgotten about that pose no threat, the spaces under the surface of stone. Go underground. I tried to converse with the man who served my tapas and he waved me away.

I grew up bilingual, speaking French at school and English at home. My friends and I invented Franglish, a dialect particular to our borderline. We spoke it, happy to be not understood, in order to be not understood. When more of our schoolwork was integrated into the English program, we abandoned Franglish. It was so easy, that way.

I boarded a bus out of the valleys, then another, for Pamplona to see the running of the bulls. I stumbled off the bus in Pamplona into a city of people dressed in white and red, carrying bottles of wine in the streets, raucous sourceless action, air made of tambourines.

Bulls coursed through my dreams all night and I bought a mountain sweater to keep me warm when I slept with the flocks of tourists in the park. Pamplona was flooded for the week-long festival. In the line-up at the internet café, the woman behind me, a Londoner, was crying and told me there had been terrorist attacks in London. Death counts still oscillating. I can't not be there right now, she told me. This is how loss cannot be separated from space. As I passed through one town to the next, carved my route southward through Spain, I took only busses and daylight rides, watched the country pass by, as if I needed to con-

Bulls Coursed Through My Dreams All Night

firm the distance I was covering, see it go. This is how I would reconfigure: through the steady covering of space, the disappearing of miles from the map in my pocket.

I perched on a post behind the double fence that kept the bulls on course. The sharp wood dug into my butt during the painful hour I perched there to keep my spot. Then: the bulls were past and gone in a second. A surge of muscle, thick faces urging forward, dirt packing, men drunk on sangria and wine lurching among the pack. I yelled hoarsely into the noise of the bulls, my English bouncing off the Spanish around me, disappearing into the run.

Hearing my accent, Spaniards asked me for days if I was English. Londoners were the Westerners of the tragic moment. I responded no, Canadian, no, Vancouver. Relieved nods. I answered questions about Vancouver. Yes, it's very beautiful. One of the best cities in the world? I don't know, I grew up there, so I don't know. Where are you going? Travelling. No, not just Pamplona. Going farther south, wherever. Just going.

Madrid's squares spread out like a flagstone carpet, boundaries drafted with elegant spire-like trees and wrought-iron benches. The city had been made Spain's capital because of its central location: jammed into the country's navel like an electrical plug, road-wires of commerce running out in all directions. I spent my nights club-hopping with Paul, a stocky thirty-something construction worker from Australia. We both wanted to drink well and late, so we got along.

I sucked tiny glasses glowing bright green, iron, yellow back into me and the club music thudded to the plan of the bull's run, the bus's lurch, the mountainous bends of Castilian. Paul and I exchanged stories. He had been moving around Australia since he left home at sixteen, forced out by the shredded energies of an abusive household. This was his first time out of Australia and he planned to find work the same way he did back home. Every time he arrived in a new city, he took a long walk and scanned the skyline for cranes, then followed the sign until he found the construction site. He could do anything with his hands, he told me, and I believed him, watched him dance in the darkness of clubs like he was building a compact, complicated building around him. I answered his questions about my trip carefully. Travelling alone. No set plan. That's some short notice you left on, honey. I explained about the heat and colour of Spain, and wanting some of that pushed into my Vancouver skin. Like being branded. A vigorous nod of agreement. He had been on the move for over a decade, because of his work but more it was the unsettledness, staying in between. The jobs he had been injured on were in the places he had felt most connected to. He showed me a scar on his leg, from an accident on a site in the town where he first fell in love. A white scar the shape of a shovel, a piece of skin to dig with.

A drink of beer, then, So what are you running from? Our laughter was the laughter of guilty travellers, laughter tugging itself apart. Laughter that had nothing to do with humour.

Paul had a daughter in Australia. Drinking later, he said he saw her so rarely that sometimes he felt like he had made her up. Her photograph had been in the wallet he had lost. Hopefully her mother would email or fax another. I felt uncomfortable listening to these confessions from a stranger, slur-faced with alcohol.

We separated after three or four days, neither of us suggesting an exchange of email addresses. Paul said that he was thinking of going back to Australia after his visa ran out.

The walls and folded roads of Toledo as I walked up into it. Wrapped sheets of stone like the layers of a blocky rose. Bullet marks left by the civil war pockmarked the high buildings of the small town. Marks from the separate reigns of the Jews, the Mores and the Christians. According to my guidebook it was a town "soaked in culture"—meaning it was a town that had been destroyed again and again by different forces held together by scars of stone. Through this war and that war, all the wars that turned something into skin and dirt. The space asked me, Do you want to end up like this? The next morning, another bus, Toledo sent me reeling further southward toward the ocean and the top of Africa. The town receded, a wound in the resilient blue of the horizon, the pale brown fields collapsing around it.

NAVIGATING CUSTOMS

Alex Leslie

In Madrid there had been a bullfight.

I climbed to a seat high on the side of the open-air stadium with my coke, sat in a smiling row with four new friends from the hostel. Cheers from the crowd, the first circuit of the toreadors in their flashing suits. I cheered and clapped with the crowd. The bull was released into the ring and launched confidently over the large pale brown round. I did not know that in a traditional bullfight the bull is killed and I leaned forward, sipping my coke. The first spike entered the bull's back and I watched it with incomprehension. Needing to confirm the realness of the wound, I picked up my camera and zoomed all the way in, just in time to see the second blade cut into the bull's dark, sweeping shoulder that filled the lens like the meat of a throbbing planet. The fight went on and I struggled to leave. I felt my body lock itself to my seat, overpowered by the cheering of the crowd, the sight of the giant animal beginning to lunge and stagger, the awful dance of a powerful thing that cannot defend itself against an unworthy opponent, the spreading possibilities of pain. Young children sat with their families, there on a weekend night to watch the bull die. I realised that I would not be able to leave until the fight was over and the bull was dead.

The toreador sprinkled the bull's back with knives—blades of different sizes that butterflied its lush skin. The knives dug deeper as the bull tried to sway them free. Its death progressed at the silent centre of the theatrics, the flashy routines of the toreador, and my own silence became deafening to myself. Finally, with a few short, strong stabs of a small knife to its head, a toreador completed the

Bulls Coursed Through My Dreams All Night

performance. Catcalls and cheers whirpooled up the walls of the stadium, waves of adoration crashing upwards and folding back down onto the bloodied ground. The bull's huge, limp body was dragged in a victory lap around the ring by a horse, then out of sight.

I rushed from my seat, tripped down the steep narrow stadium steps into the warm nighttime air. I thought about bombs as I sat waiting in the subway tunnel for the next train.

The next day I left for Toledo, where the violence could be sensed, folded back into itself, wrapped into the stone and lost in its cycles, the stone never being its own stone, just battered, passed, from one war to the next. After Toledo there was another sweaty bus ride and Cordoba, where tourists filled a mosque that the Christians had captured and built in a small cathedral inside its black-and-orange striped belly. A statue of Jesus hung against a backdrop of gold, cast in gloom against the remaining mosque walls, like a second gilded heart transplanted into a still-beating body. Farther and farther South. Granada dominated by the ancient Alhambra palace. Malaga and the stamps of Picasso's birthplace, blue shadow paintings of cubist rooms and dead friends. Last, Algeciras, a port town sliding off the chin of Spain, full of backpackers, pickpockets, the boat-noises of ferries leaving for Morocco every hour on the hour. I boarded a ferry for Tangier, across the Strait of Gibraltar, listened to Moroccan children converse in French on the ride over, a language both the same as mine and a whole language away from my soft-tongued west coast Canadian French.

NAVIGATING CUSTOMS

Alex Leslie

Europe slid away, painted across the ridge of waves. The air dipped into ripple-tides of cool across the smooth dark-blue water, then heated with the oncoming ridge of Africa. Bright eyes, cracked hot stone. The main square in Marrakech swarmed with women offering henna, vendors selling orange juice who began to yell when I was twenty feet away, cotton sheets spread with human teeth, knots of dried herbs, cracked amulets, tangles of shining anklets. I tossed back glass after glass of the orange juice, flicking the flies off my lips, the taste cleaning my mouth out like heat, sharp and complete. Here, Vancouver was a surreal memory, a watercolour city, a place bathed in a blue hand that you stood in the palm of, looking up at the distant overreaching fingers like the dark Pacific mountains. Marrakech was a burning slate of brown, pink, red, mustard. Here, I had reached the fire, and finally I let it burn right through me.

A train carried me back across the country from Marrakech to Tangier. I bought a third-class ticket, sat on the hard seats in a small compartment in the back of the train, shared with two Moroccans, one a young man who passed around pastries in sealed plastic bags, one an elderly man who smiled largely, who wore a coarse white cotton shirt that stood out startlingly against his brown skin. Unlike Paul, with his small builder's body, this man was languidly built, his elegant frame undiminished by age. He stretched his thin legs in front of him, flattened his worn sandals against the floor, began speaking. The train did not suit him, he said. He had been a sailor. Tangier had once been an international zone, the nexus of his voyages – he was fluent in English, French, Spanish, Arabic, Portuguese and Italian. It was impossible to determine from his sun-cured skin and hard pale eyes which language was his first, which country he could call home. Canada? No, he had never been there, except for once during the Second World War. A boat trip to Quebec, where the boat had been turned away and sent back. I listened to this story silently – the only story I heard during my trip that I did not pursue for more details. I remembered learning in a history class years before about the boatloads of Jews who were sent back, and thinking how the ocean was the only safe space for them, the vast in-between area without ports or endings, where stopping meant death.

I fell asleep and woke up to two Moroccan women yelling at the elderly man beside me, who had been fiercely defending the two unoccupied seats I was lying across while I slept. I sat up and the women immediately zipped into the seats, like magnets. The young man across from me grinned and leaned forward.

"You have no idea how many people he fought off while you were asleep."

Tangier in the morning was thick with warm dust. The boat back to Spain and then a bus to Lisbon, where my trip would end. I took the map out of my pouch, where it was folded safely with my airplane ticket and passport, and drew on the final leg I was about to travel, across the thick pale gray borderline into Portugal. There I would be surrounded again by European architecture: none of the crooked streets and off-kilter lines of Morocco, none of that purity of heat and light, everything stained a bright inside-eyelid red. In Lisbon, small boys played accordion on the street, accompanied by tiny dogs gripping money pouches in their teeth. I dissolved once again into the newness of a place, the last of the places that had ridden through me—a kind of colonisation. I gathered these places together, fragments of remembered ocean, hostels, drinks, paintings, instruments, faces, and pieced them together into a map I could manage to navigate. From Lisbon to Vancouver, I drew the last line home.

Zarmina Rafi *is a graduate student at Concordia University, Montréal. She is currently at work on a collection of short stories.*

OF TRAVEL AND ART

IN JULY 2005, AFTER having lived in Canada for seven years, my sister and I traveled to Lahore, Pakistan, the city of my birth. Lahore is a city of ten million people and the cultural capital of Pakistan. There is a certain air about the city, an air that serves as backdrop to the honking cars, a lot of dust, blaring music, lush green trees, and trucks painted in vivid yellows and reds. The entire time we were in Lahore, my sister remained obsessed with the idea of trying to record things. She photographed constantly, what was in her way, and what was out of her way. I, aspiring to be a writer, wrote nothing—opting instead to rely upon memory. I objected to her desire of capturing our city in photographs. There was no way a picture could do that.

When this picture was taken we were standing in Anarkali Bazaar. I remember the exact moment, but perhaps it wasn't like this. My sister and I are arguing, in a narrow lane, in a crowded market. I had advised her only to speak in Urdu. I advised her not to talk in English, for the shopkeepers would raise their prices upon detecting her Canadian-accented English. I myself break the rule and start to argue with her in English. Men swarm all around, trying to sell us everything imaginable, like rows of fake designer glasses that they carry on their person, all along the length of their arms, some even attached to the front of their shirts. I had told her it was hot and noisy, claustrophobic, her picture could never say that. The picture she did take is red in the background, and shows bronze necklaces on display, with the young sales clerk standing to one side. Her picture is too calm, too evenly red. In her picture the black of the female mannequin's hair is shiny, and the lights too luminous. In it I have no beads of sweat around my neck; there is none of the expectation of the salesmen around me. The one who hopes we might make purchases worth thousands of rupees. The man who is selling peacock shaped earrings. "One pair of peacocks for every good friend," my sister says. The smaller peacocks are for roommates who have threatened to throw out her furniture by the end of the summer.

When I look at this photograph it cannot be enough to explain to the onlooker that there was heat but it was nostalgic, that there was noise but the sort of noise doesn't even exist in North America. There was color, of machines and bikes, of people bustling, and water hissing in large pots used to dye clothes. In a Lahori market one can have a length of fabric dyed to any shade of one's choosing, to make curtains or dresses or bedspreads with. Where we stood was dirty and there were little puddles, plastic bags, sugarcane juice carts and paan spit. It was the city that I grew up in. The children's bikes with painted on cartoon characters, hanging in stores, were reminiscent of childhood shopping trips with my mother. There is no way my sister could capture this noise—noise not only in its nega-

Of Travel and Art

tive connotation but in terms of combined movement and sound, in narrow lanes, rows of sandals, and high voltage bulbs illuminating cheap wares.

Knowing all this the two of us were still outsiders. I was aware that I viewed the city through the lens of where I was now coming from, and where I had been. I was a tourist but also one returning home. I was able to walk into a Western style mall; I could enjoy an expensive buffet meal, or get a haircut at a trendy salon. But once outside of these exclusive spaces, once on the streets, was I the same as all others on the street? Like them, I too was free to take in the lights along the canal road, the old city gates, the Lahore fort, the sufis, the devotees and the addicts outside the mosques. Yet I wasn't the same as them at all.

Being back in Pakistan, there was also the matter of our bodies. As children, my sister and I grew up in open spaces, but as young women we were confined in our bodies as objects. We existed in the private worlds of private school girls—our hearts belonged in Sweet Valley California, they were entwined with the lives of blue-green eyed twins from the American books that we read voraciously. But as Islamic architecture is conceived of as a regulation of symbols, in real life a similar regulation applied to our bodies in being female. We were used to walking in markets with our bodies held out as torches, aware of where our person ended, and where someone's hand, arm, finger could touch ours. In 2005, as a woman travelling through crowded spaces, I knew all the places I could not be in. These were the landscapes of men; these were roadside cafes that I could not insert myself into, except possibly through fiction. So I imagined that tea in the road side stalls tasted better, looked more authentic, and the naans and chickpea curry they passed around had to be more delicious than any other I had tasted.

Having said all that, here she was, my sister, taking pictures, taking control. My sister, seemingly Pakistani but with a very strange haircut—telling others what to do, orchestrating the actions of men and women. The shopkeepers smiled too wide. She positioned her Nikon towards them, she directed them, "no, don't smile so much," or "repeat that gesture," or in the brass market, "pick up your tools again." She asked them to look away, but not really. I wasn't sure what would come of it, to the extent that I started leaving her behind in mazelike streets. I hoped finding me gone would make her quicken her pace, forget about the orchestration of poses. But instead I had to retrace my steps and find her again. As for me, the point of the journey was to move through crowds and streets undetected, as easily as possible. In my mind my job was to observe only—say nothing, antagonize no one.

I am writing a story about a boy who is fascinated with napkins. Who feels excited but small, walking around tall buildings in a new city, and knowing his shoes are all wrong, not stylish enough, but lumpy, unwieldy, just practical-durable.

This is the second photograph in my account. A sepia one, taken in the year 1975. My father is twenty four and in Germany. I don't know much about him then, except

Of Travel and Art

that it's his first time out of Pakistan. He has sideburns, and he's wearing a leather jacket, and bell bottoms. Fresh out of engineering university, and sent across the ocean on behalf of his new job, what did my father think/feel upon landing in Stuttgart, Germany? Going from too many people to what? Landing in the city of? What does my character experience when his world has always been conceived in knowable shapes, in familiar images?

At the age of twenty four, one of the things my father would have known about Germany is that Allama Iqbal, the national poet of Pakistan, had once studied in Munich, and soon after a street was named after him, in Munich. Just as there is an airport named after Iqbal in Pakistan today. On his three week trip to Stuttgart my father would frequent a particular café. He loved that with a meal they would distribute freely, and at no cost to the customer, these large napkins, disposable squares. As he came from a primarily agricultural economy, I believe it was the throw-away aspect of these napkins that attracted him. Germany was the place where he ordered a club sandwich for the first time, triangles. He was surprised to find the toothpick in the sandwich, surprised that it was positioned to hold together the sandwich rather than to destabilize it. Adding something to food that did not belong with food, this was new. Can I put this incident into a piece of fiction? His fascination with napkins—or will someone think that all Pakistanis are fascinated with napkins? Here I pause and think why write about the traversing of worlds? Because one has to say it, state it? Because the more people hear about an unfamiliar place, the more comfortable they begin to get with the idea of that place? And perhaps one day the idea

NAVIGATING CUSTOMS

can come into contact with the place itself, at which point the reader can decide what was real, what unreal, the end result being a possible point of entry into an alien place, as an alien being.

One of the few purchases my father made in Germany was a small electric kettle for his father. Of course that was a silly thing to do, he recounts much later. Because there would never be just one cup of tea, there would always be a crowd, and they would drink a fresh pot every hour. Also, my grandfather would never make tea for himself. The women of the household would cater to that. So the concept of tea for one, and dining for one, remained a failed idea in my father's hometown, Okara, Pakistan.

On the same trip to Germany, my father met some Germans who had traveled to Pakistan previously. They invited him over for a traditional Pakistani meal, cooked daal and rice for him. How would this have tasted to him? A traditional meal of daal and rice, how did he approach it there? Was it his food but not the same?

My father always talks of food and seasons like complimentary colours. For him, growing up in Pakistan, a rainy day always meant eating pakoras. His relation to the country was based on ties to the physical land, and so the way of living was abundant, with no containment. In Canada now, for my father there is an experience of compartmentalization, an alien sense present in the rituals of daily life. When my mother and he have alternating work schedules, he finds this way of silently eating in an empty house strange, this way of portioning food cold and

Of Travel and Art

mechanical. Is the project of art to make connections, to some degree move outside of the compartmentalization and division of categories?

Having been to Pakistan recently I wish to write controlled narrations like cut glass, because the experience overwhelms me, and I must find a way to contain it. Regarding the aesthetics of our respective work, my sister and I are in agreement now. In agreement that it should be clean and stark. For the moment this is our conclusion, the starkness being a distillation of a past rush, of having lived within some other momentum.

At the same time I have in my possession photographs that I can touch, twist and bend. I can expand upon the shopkeeper standing under a yellow light in the photograph, clad in a cotton shalwar kameez, a pocket on the left side of his kameez, and in my mind all the markets of Lahore converge to make a singular market. Similarly, the picture of my father in bell bottoms, in Germany, offers a corner that I can claim as mine, and that I am free to fictionalize.

I transpose the story about my father in Germany onto a story about a young man's first trip to Canada. In the fictional story a young man moves from a village in Pakistan to the suburbs of Toronto, Canada. He gains employment as a factory labourer. He wears unflattering shoes, both because of the physical nature of his work, and because he doesn't own a better pair. By day he works to save up money, and at night he dreams of visiting the home he has left behind. One night he dreams he is at home and his sisters and cousins are gathered around him. They are waiting in anticipation, as he brings out a brown suitcase with a blue lining, a suitcase full of presents. They come closer, and when he opens the suitcase it is filled with large white napkins, and napkins keep coming.

Born in 1985, **Fenn Elan Stewart** *writes where she lives—with Pearl and often Anton, upstairs, in a small house and a fine chaos in Vancouver, British Columbia.*

YA IDU, BLYAD

THE FIRST PART OF travelling is leaving, right?

Nu Da, so I will tell you a story about leaving.

Da said, What about love, then?

She said, I don't know. Love is maybe the white stains that flower on boot-leather all winter. Love is maybe creaking aisle seats and a rising terror in your throat but you do it anyway. Love is maybe streets you don't walk down and markets you avoid.

I was introduced to the country by a man who loved it passionately.

His mother was born there—grew up there. She left in her twenties. She flew to a new, green country where she taught her sons to pronounce their names and fed them the food she ate as a child. When I knew him, I fell in love with the country myself. I breathed fragrant smoke, I read the books, I listened to the music. I sat on the floor, eyes half-closed and humming, as he and his friends argued. I loved the language as much as I couldn't understand it.

NAVIGATING CUSTOMS

I grew tired of the man—and the country—and when, a year and a half later, I met another man from the same place, I had lost interest all together.

Imagine, Da, a back street downtown in a city. Three men lean against a door, waiting in the cold sun. There's a tall one with drooping black hair. He's thin and wears tight jeans and a hoodie. There's a short one with dreadlocks and finally, that one. He smokes and shivers and shakes his hair out of his eyes.

The truck pulls in. A small man jumps out, shakes hands with the blond giant who's just arrived from inside. They shake hands and slap each other on the back.

The unloading begins. Each of the three loads his dolly up with boxes, wheels it in the side door. This is the back room. Piles of rotting fruit, boxes with black ooze dripping from the bottom, fruit flies so thick you're breathing and eating and chewing them every time you open your mouth. Have you ever eaten fruit flies, Da? I wouldn't recommend it.

You walk past the tiny garbage elevator. There's a thin kid inside, knee deep in sprouting potatoes. He's pale and doesn't know how to shave. He's taking the garbage up to the compactor. His name is probably Alexei.

Inside, where it's warm, the huge blond man is talking to a girl. She's looking for a job. He yells "YOULIA!" across the store. "You start now," he tells the girl, and walks off.

Ya Idu, Blyad

Youlia, beautiful and redhaired and wearing tiny jeans, appears.

"*Salut*," she says, sighing. "*Je m'appelle Youlia, et je ne parle pas anglais.*"

"*Moi non plus,*" adds a man, as he passes by with a giant box of pineapples.

"*C'est une langue vraiment laide. Vous, anglophones, vouz parlez comme BLARGH BLARGH BLARGH.*"

He smiles suddenly; his face breaks into a million lines.

Youlia has meanwhile found a large box of zucchini that needs to be put away.

"*S'il vous plaît, serrez les courgettes.*"

Youlia stalks off on four-inch heels and the new girl grabs the box.

She looks around her at a giant maze of fruits and vegetables. Mad grandmothers lug quadruple-bagged cabbage. A small woman with a thick Jamaican accent argues about bananas.

Towering oranges. Piles of coconuts. Every few minutes one of these falls to the floor and bounces off with a loud cracking noise.

In the midst of this, Evgeni pulls his dolly through the aisle. He slows down as he passes the new girl, and a head of broccoli falls to the floor. Dropping her box of zucchini, the girl hands his broccoli back.

He takes it without thanking her. He looks tired and his hair's too long. He frowns.

"Are you working here?"

She thinks she knows his accent.

"Yeah," she answers, "I just started. Listen—I have a question—" She digs into the box of zucchini and pulls one out to show him. "Can you tell me where these are supposed to go?"

He stares at her for a few seconds, eyebrows crinkled. He shakes his head, and smiles. "Really?" He walks off, pushing through a crowd of people scrabbling for half-priced fava beans.

I can see you there, Da. You'd like it. Smoking on the patio, maybe, with the sparrows. Groups of old men used to sit there, and when we'd walk by they'd whistle, and offer to buy us coffee.

Now listen Da, it's years later. Monday morning, downtown. A different city. The sky is grey. The pavement is grey. Just look, Da—the wind's blowing hard and, across the street, a woman's umbrella is trying to escape. These two aren't paying attention. They're looking at their shoes moving, at the curb as they cross it, at each other.

Up the stairs and through the door in their long dark coats.

Ya Idu, Blyad

The elevator rises. A trio of civil servants stare, and mutter to each other in their secret language. The air smells like too many exhales at once.

They walk out of the elevator, when—right there—so close you could touch them: two men in Guantanamo orange, hands cuffed in front, shuffling, yes, actually shuffling, down the hall towards the elevator.

The men don't look up—they're guided along the grey carpet by two guards. At the sight of them the couple stares, first at the orange, then at each other, and the stare means, yes, these men just walked out of the office we're walking into, what's wrong with us, are we fucking crazy, if we have any sense we'll turn quickly and walk out of this building and go home as fast as we can, to the cat and the fish and the clothes on the floor of our room, and we'll climb into bed, and pull the blankets over our heads, and just not think about this anymore. Ok? Ok.

But they walk in anyway, without glancing back. They sit on hard chairs and begin to make uncomfortable jokes. Perhaps these men have been hired by the government to intimidate immigrants, perhaps they have a union, dental plans. Cuffed-and-suited convict to guard:

"And Joe, can I offer a little constructive criticism? If you don't shove me a little while I'm stepping into the elevator it's just not believable."

The waiting room is an irregular shape. The walls make thin angles near the corners.

NAVIGATING CUSTOMS

Behind bulletproof glass the receptionists sit, sipping tea.

Two women speak at the same time into the tiny voice holes:

"I realise that, I realise that, but we don't even know where he's being held."

"We just want to know where he's being held."

Feedback—a tinny voice—

"Ma-am—ma-am—I've already told you—he's not being held here. There's nothing I can do. You'll have to fax a letter through –"

Evgeni is busy remembering how to breathe. He tells Sally that you can tell how bad the news will be by how empty the room is. Sometimes, apparently, people want to throw things at civil servants.

And the room is empty. On the desk there's only a box of Kleenex and a giant Polaroid-style camera. After the introductions are made, and eight pictures of Evgeni appear, all three sit.

The woman across the desk has extremely large eyes. She speaks in a whispery voice, as though the news will hurt less if it's delivered quietly.

"So I'm afraid the paperwork I have here indicates that…" She squints to read his name. "Ev—Evgeni—is going to have to leave. Of course, how long he's gone depends,

Ya Idu, Blyad

to a certain extent, on you two...On how quickly you manage to file once he leaves..."

"I'm sorry," she says, removing her glasses and folding her hands. "There's just no way around it."

When I'm asked I explain, apologetically, that my trip isn't really a holiday—a family crisis, I explain. Da, I don't want to go. It's my own fault, isn't it, Da?

You would have known better—would never have expected so much. People steal rotten pears from the backroom. People are paid under the table so the boss doesn't have to pay minimum... People are arrested and made to wear orange and made to shuffle. And there are women with big eyes and a whispery voices—and, I forgot to tell you, Da, a big fat diamond on her ring finger—whose job it is to tell you that he has to go, there's nothing you can do, no good reason why, and she is so sorry. And so you have to go, too.

NAVIGATING CUSTOMS

Gillian Sze *was raised in Winnipeg, Manitoba. She has been published in The University of Winnipeg Creative Writing Journal,* Juice, *as well as Concordia's* Headlight Anthology. *In 2004, she received the University of Winnipeg Writers' Circle Prize. Her first chapbook,* This is the Colour I Love You Best, *was published by Withwords Press in 2007. She is currently pursuing her Master's degree in Creative Writing and resides in Montréal.*

ROOFTOP

THE STREETLIGHTS BELOW OFFERED little colour that early morning. Maya stood on the roof of her 20-storey apartment and stared at the row of glimmering yellow against the backdrop of downtown Montréal. She wondered how she always found herself elevated, looking down at the tops of heads. She had seen many hats, bald spots, whorls and parts in her twenty-one years. Climbing, like how others sucked their thumbs, was her source of comfort carried on from childhood. The earliest of these times that she could recall was when she was eight. Her parents had been fighting all day. She could not remember about what, but after the smash of the third dinner plate, she had opened her window and held onto the tree branch that extended straight to the roof of her bungalow in Gimli. She scrambled up while hearing words that she'd never heard before, then sat there on the roof, observing how the sky turned black, and listening to her house turn quiet. That night, Maya had sat watching the boys who lived across the street toss a football with their friends. They were just shadows and silhouettes with baseball caps and loud voices. She watched the dark figures prance in the street, disappearing behind trees, and then peeking out through the moonlight. After the boys slipped back into the house, and the engine of the truck carrying their friends turned the corner at the end of the road, she could hear different sounds coming from her parents' room below her. She listened to them make love for the last time before they announced a few days later that they were getting a divorce.

It had been three years since Maya left Gimli. She and Leif had finished high school that spring, and spent their afternoons parked in the far fields of his family's farm. They'd sit in the back of his pickup truck, smoking stolen cigarettes and writing songs. She had taught him how to blow smoke rings, and he had tried to teach her chords. "Can't you hold down all the strings?" he'd ask, pressing her forefinger close to the fret board. They both knew that she couldn't, but he always asked. In the end, she had given up and never learned how to play the guitar. Leif, as Maya learned yesterday when he showed up unexpectedly at her door, had picked up smoking as if he always had a cigarette between his fingers – long before Maya had lit his first one.

"I thought you'd be up here."

Maya turned around to see Leif standing at the door, one hand on the knob. He was wearing what he wore last night when he arrived at her apartment, torn jeans and the blue plaid shirt that she had always teased him about when they were younger. Farm boy, she would call him. Beauty, he'd reply. His wheat-coloured hair lay tumbled on one side and Maya thought he looked just as he did

Rooftop

when they were fourteen, awkward and fumbling in his parents' basement.

"I hope I didn't wake you," Maya said. His six-foot frame looked small before the expanse of the city with its layers of buildings and glass windows. She could make out the edge of the island behind him, and the small surrounding mountains.

Leif knew that something was wrong. Maya only went to rooftops when something was wrong. Like after finding out her father had died because his heart had suddenly stopped, or that last morning when she decided to leave her mom and her drunken boyfriend and follow whatever her thumb could catch.

Once when they were fifteen, he had climbed the tree outside her window in the middle of the night, only to realize that her bed was empty. He eventually found her on the roof. They had had sex for the first time earlier that day and she had cried. She said she was scared of the blood. On her roof, he had taken her hand, and she had turned to him to say, "It feels like shutting a door, and I can't have anything keeping me here, do you know what I mean?"

Last night, Maya came home late from bartending and was deluded that she would sleep well. The phone next to her bed suddenly rang. She heard a voice that made her automatically poke her head under her sheets and whisper, "Where are you?", like she did a long time ago when phone calls after ten would mean a hard knock on her bedroom door.

NAVIGATING CUSTOMS

"In the lobby," Leif replied.

"As in downstairs in the lobby?"

"Yeah."

Maya recalled the letter she had sent him last month, the first one that included her return address. After it was stamped and sealed, she had looked at it and noticed her Montréal location printed neatly at the top left hand corner. She didn't remember writing it, or why she didn't white it out, but she regretted it now. She thought it strange that this prairie boy was standing in the lobby of her apartment with busy streets encompassing the building. For a moment, she wondered if she could get away with pretending that he had buzzed the wrong apartment.

"So are you gonna let me up?" he asked.

Maya rubbed her eyes. "Yeah, hold on."

When she heard the knock, Maya took a deep breath and opened her door. There was Leif in the hallway, his guitar strapped to his back and a duffel bag in one hand. He ducked his head and smiled. It was familiar and though she had been dreading this moment from the time she hung up the phone, she felt an unexpected relief when she saw him.

Leif was surprised that Maya was wearing only a long shirt. Her hair, once short as a boy's, had grown past her shoulders. It wasn't the red that he remembered—the same shade as a fox—instead, it had become brown and dull. She

Rooftop

looked tired but she smiled and said, "I thought you'd only go as far as writing me back, Leif Anderson."

White bed sheets hung forgotten, wet from last night's rain. To Maya's left, buildings stood grey and silent, the masses of concrete blending in with the mist that hovered along the skyline. Leif approached her and asked, "Is everything okay?" He knew that she wouldn't say.

"I'm fine. When do you have to leave again?"

"Quarter to ten." Up here was the highest he'd ever been, and though Leif wasn't at the edge of the roof where there were no rails, he kept his hand close to the chimneys and ducts. When he reached her, he grasped her arm and brought her closer to him. Her hair smelled of shampoo. It mingled with the damp air and the faint scent of laundry.

After Leif had entered Maya's apartment, they quickly fell back into their old ways: the way they hugged with her arms around his waist and his arms closer to her shoulders, the tossing of shoes into the corner, the sighs when falling back into the couch. There had been some moments of unease like when Leif told her that her mother was still with Sam, and that there were days when she never left the house. She had turned quiet, and when he bumped into her at the grocery store, she would only smile softly and chitchat briefly about the weather or the season, before making a swift exit.

Maya had stiffened and told Leif that she didn't want to hear about Gimli and her mother. "Tell me what you're doing," she said.

NAVIGATING CUSTOMS

Leif told her about the friends he had met when he started Red River College in Winnipeg. They had formed a band and began opening shows for other bands from Manitoba. "We're just starting out, but it's exciting as hell," he told her. "When I found out that we were driving out here to play, I grabbed your letter and nearly forgot everything else. I would've called earlier but I didn't have your number."

Maya didn't tell Leif about the people she had met on the way to Montréal, like the men who didn't just give free rides, or the parks that she had fallen asleep in on the way out east. She knew that Leif would only be troubled by it. So she told him about how she had stayed at hostels, learned to wash her clothes in sinks, and even bathed in someone's backyard pool. Maya had come into Montréal with an acquaintance she had met at church, who was returning to the big city. It wasn't long before acquaintances became friends, and she found herself working at a pub downtown where tips weren't the greatest but did the job.

They talked about the three years, skipping over the subjects they knew Maya didn't want to talk about, until the two spoke with their eyes closed. Maya eventually got up and stretched. "I'm going to bed now, I'll grab you some blankets, I guess."

"Yeah, sure, thanks," Leif said, looking around at the couch.

Later, lying in bed, Maya looked up at the ceiling and listened to Leif arrange the blankets around him, and then re-arrange them again. It was silent until she heard a knock on the wall. Leif was standing in her doorway in the dark.

"I can't sleep," he said.

"I know. I can't either."

"Could I—"

"Yeah."

He circled to her side of the bed and slipped in. He smelled of the past, of oats and sweat and Leif. They didn't do anything except hold each other and listen to each other breathe, just as they did back home when they snuck into each other's bedrooms in the middle of the night and sleep was far away and hard to reach.

Now Maya stood staring at the wet gravel by her feet and listened to the sound of the garbage truck below her start and stop again. Each jolt of the engine almost sounded like the beginning of a symphony. The men's voices bounced off the walls of the buildings, reaching her ears in a distorted sound of static.

The two were quiet for a while. Maya leaned against Leif's body and remembered how her mother had screamed that she didn't care Maya was leaving. That she would come crawling back. Maya had shouted back that she'd rather die first. Before she left, she had almost asked Leif to come with her, but she knew that he wouldn't. He had both his parents, an older brother studying engineering in the city, a neatly wall-papered kitchen and a loyal border collie named Barkley.

Leif finally spoke. "How about after I reach the east coast, and we come back this way again, I'll take you with me. Back to Gimli." The sun coming up gave the buildings a washed-up yellow tinge.

Maya didn't say anything, just looked straight ahead at the city sprawl.

He let his hands drop from her body and stuffed them into his pockets. "What do you say?"

Maya looked at him. He was as tall as when she left him, but there was something about Leif that was bigger, wider, and so much of what she remembered. He studied her face and she tugged at the ends of her hair. "I can't go."

Leif looked down while shuffling the gravel with the toe of his shoe, then glanced up at her quickly before asking, "Why not?"

In the distance, she could hear sirens. She wondered what could've happened so early in the morning. Maya bit her lip. "I just can't. I haven't seen her in years. I wouldn't be able to just... show up."

"Of course you would—she's your mother."

"Leif, I didn't leave as her daughter." He looked at her confused, and she didn't know how to explain that last night in Gimli. The yelling, the words *I hate you*, the

Rooftop

wishes for death and never-been-born. There was the final slap to Maya's face, the echoes in the front hallway.

Leif swallowed and looked up at the sky. "Right. You just left." He looked back down at her. "Maya, when you took off, you didn't just take off on your mother, you took off on me too. You didn't even tell me," his voice rose, "you came by like it was just another ordinary day. And then I get letters that leave out all the important things—like why you didn't want me to come, where you were, or if you were ever coming back."

"I left it all there," Maya replied. "I couldn't just ask you to come—you had the farm, your family—I needed to go. You knew what it was like at home—"

"But what about us?"

"We were seventeen!" Maya retorted. "You'd been my boyfriend since the eighth grade! You would never have hurt me, and maybe at seventeen I wanted someone who could have."

He stared at her and felt like he did that day he watched her leave with her blue and white knapsack draped over one arm. Sound travelled slowly that morning. He had watched her open and close the gate, and it was only when she was gone, far down the road, that he heard the jingle of the catch.

Maya suddenly looked different to him. Despite last night and the comfort that they had had together, she had changed. It could have happened when she had her thumb in the wind, or when she found herself in this city so different from where she was born. Leif didn't know the exact moment—it could've even been as early as that summer three years ago when Maya put down his guitar, looked at him and said solemnly, "I quit"—but he could see that she wasn't going back, not with him.

He reached over and tucked a strand of brown hair behind her ear. He had never done that before, and it felt strange, but oddly comforting. Her eyes were wet and she tried to smile.

"Ok," he said. The questions he had carried with him didn't matter anymore. Time hadn't stopped that day she left. He saw that now. There was no answer that would change or undo anything. He looked down at his watch.

"So I guess I'll see you," he paused, "when I come back this way?"

"Yes, I'd like that," Maya said. She meant it. She glanced at the door behind them and realized that she felt like going back down.

Leif left the apartment and headed to the hotel where his friends were staying. The sun had come up and the concrete walls of the buildings around him were half-dry. He pulled his cap lower and then looked up at Maya's window. Sure enough, she was leaning out, her weight resting on both elbows. She wasn't close enough to reach over and kiss like when he was dangling upside

Rooftop

down from a tree, branch hooked in the bend of his legs, but she was close enough for him to see her bring a hand to her mouth and blow.

NAVIGATING CUSTOMS

*Born and raised in Montréal, **Talia Weisz** is wrapping up her B.A. double major in Creative Writing and Anthropology at Concordia University. Her hobbies include singing in the shower, eating toast with almond butter, and fiddling with words. She is deeply grateful to her family for their support, encouragement, and love.*

KUPE'S VOYAGE AND OTHER STORIES

GREAT BARRIER ISLAND

Great Barrier Island was once attached
to the rest of New Zealand.
Now it drifts on the South Pacific
like a disembodied head.

>It's that easy: step on a plane
>and you are wrenched from gravity's pull.
>You hurtle through space like a meteor.

>A scrawled note
>rolled up
>stuffed in an empty beer bottle
>cast to sea.

1897. Great Barrier Island's first pigeon postal service.
Courier birds released across the Hauraki gulf.
Bound to their legs:
mine claims, election results and news.
Now it's a tourist novelty.

NAVIGATING CUSTOMS

Talia Weisz

Pigeons are ordered from Auckland by ferry.
For twenty dollars you can release one with a message.
They fly back to Auckland
every time.

You are made of water and you will fly over water,
Juan wrote before I left. *I offer to you*
two useful implements.
Here is a bag. It is for holding things.
Inside you will find something for holding thoughts.

> A lonely beach.
> Pohutukawa trees
> lean twisted along the shore.
> I drift, a wisp of dandelion.
> A man turned to the sea,
> tendrils of his beard in the wind.
> Us two
> side by side,
> two twigs so brittle they could snap
> in a gust.
> Behind us,
> A tree half uprooted.
> An icy chill.
> *Winter's not yet gone.*
> His teeth
> rotting at the gums.
>
> *Sure is cold.*

His eyes
two glass marbles.
Worse down south.
Hurricane blew a house clean over.
Killed the lady and her boy,
found them under the rubble.
Last month a backpacker
died on Mount Cook.
Frozen solid.
Strokes his beard
thoughtfully.
Walks away.

>Hermit crabs make their homes
>in abandoned shells.
>Empty cabins, each one
>exactly like the last.
>Bare walls, cracked ceilings
>faded bedspreads, I linger
>in each doorway. Can't decide
>which one to claim.

I phone Juan in Montréal.
His Canadian Visa expires in a month.
His voice echoes across a chasm.
I dreamed about you.

>*What was I like?*

We were at the beach.

NAVIGATING CUSTOMS

Talia Weisz

You wore a bikini.

                        Tears streaming down my face.
                        How else was I?

    A shower of static.
                    Juan? Juan?

                        Walking back to my cabin
                        I find a glass bottle
                        smashed on the rocks.

Juan's father trained
in the Mexican Air Force at seventeen.
At eighteen he leapt out the window of his parents' home
and bounded through the courtyard
towards the open gate.
1945. He was joining the war.
His mother hanging out the window.
Don't leave without saying goodbye!

    1949. He crash-landed in the Sonoran desert.
    Broken wings. No food.
    Just his jack-knife and Colt .45.

Juan gave me a woven knapsack.
Inside, a notebook of soft handmade paper.
I took neither with me. I was a seed
stripped of its husk.
            That night he whispered
            I release you.

He meant to sound poetic.
I walked away from him
like I was stepping off the edge
                of the earth.

Bad luck to fall
in love before a journey.
October 29, 1894.
SS Wairarapa shipwrecked
on the rocky shores of Great Barrier Island.
A hole ripped in the hull, water flooded in.
The steamer tilted to one side.
Passengers and crew sliding off the deck
into the sea,
some climbed to the bridge.
Wave smashed the bridge
and swept them away.

Currach Pub. Tables stand like silent trees.
The Pohutukawas will flower in summer,
a spray of crimson igniting the coast.
I've seen pictures.
Now
their skeleton spines
bent with longing.

A reversal of seasons.
When I left
summer was trickling away.

NAVIGATING CUSTOMS

Talia Weisz

Sparrows alighting on the telephone wires.
They always know where to go,
always know when it's time.

Hokianga

I

Kupe, chief of Hawaiki
set sail one morning.
His family and crew in two waka canoes.
A hunt for the octopus Te Wheke-o-Muturangi
whose children stole the bait off the fishermens' hooks.
Two waka racing south into colder seas,
read glow of their prey
below the surface of the water.
Weeks flowed by. Te Wheke swam on.
But look: a long white cloud on the horizon.
Behind it, a shore.
They cornered Te Wheke in a cave
birthing young. Smashed the walls in.
Te Wheke,
240 feet long
24 feet wide
snapped their spears in two,
seized hold of Kupe's canoe.
With a mighty blow of the axe
Kupe struck her in the eyes.

Te Wheke sank.
They chanted karakia
so that none could revive her.
Sailed the contours of the land.
Two islands, separated by a narrow strait.
O, Kupe! Let us take possession of it.
A feast was held in the northern hills.
Kupe named the place Hokianga: to return
From here they departed, bound for home
saddled with riches: dried moa meat,
pounamu greenstone.
Their people crowded round the boats.
O Kupe! What does it look like?
Cloud-capped, mountains rise, plains unfold.
Soil rich and black.
Were there people?
Only birds, whistling in the gullies.
What is the way?
South, to the right of the setting sun.

II

Group by group
Kupe's descendents sailed here
over hundreds of years.
Aotearoa: *land of the long white cloud*

1973. Marina, age fifteen
arrived from Germany with her lover
intending never to return.

NAVIGATING CUSTOMS

Talia Weisz

She comes to meet me at Hokianga harbour.
Hills rise to meet the clouds.
She steps out of her car in a man's plaid shirt,
her hands dry and cracked. Wraps me in a hug
as though I've come home.

III

Steamed windows, simmering pots.
Marina's husband Daniel, weathered and wiry,
eyes twinkling with secrets.
Two others, young like me.
Holly from Ireland, moon-faced, silent.
Sonja, a German, wide-eyed as a frightened hare.
We peel garlic, chop potatoes, eager to help,
dreading stillness.
At the table, steal glances at each other.
Forks clink. Rain batters the roof.
You've all come a long way to get here.
We nod. Look away.

When Marina and her man found this place
it was mud and bush. Soil hard clay.
They cleared trees, forged gardens.
When he left she remained,
raised five kids in an old caravan.
Two dogs now inhabit it.

Relics abound like washed-up seashells.
Sandbox under a tree bough, pail and shovel half-buried.

Two shacks in the field, former homes
of teens now grown.
One boasts a sign, *Only Babes Allowed*.
The path to the doorstep is a mosaic of tiles,
colours dancing, polished by rain.
The work of travelers come and gone.

Mornings I wake to birdsong, intricate melodies
lost in the breeze.
Wisps of my life like curling smoke, dreams dissolving
in the chilly air.

We fix our breakfasts, absorbed
in the ritual of our chosen foods.
Oatmeal. Toast. Peanut butter. Sliced apple.
A silent meditation. Inside our shells, we are tender.
All around us, hills rise. Valley open like a bruise.

IV

In the beginning: Maui the demi-god.
Youngest of six brothers, too young to fish with them.
One day, he hid in the bottom of their waka.
Out at sea, they discovered him
and turned the boat around.
Maui, a trickster: made the shoreline appear to recede
as they drew near.
They gave up. Paddled towards the horizon,
threads of his laughter in the wind.
In deep ocean, he cast a line with his magic fishhook.

Talia Weisz

Felt a powerful tug. With his brothers
    he heaved
    rope strained
    Te Ika surfaced writhing.
    Fish of Maui -   he clubbed it
    hills and valleys
    its body an island.

Te Ika a Maui — North Island
Te Waka a Maui — South Island
Te Punga a Maui — Stewart Island, the anchor

V

Sonja shows me postcards of her village.
Pointed steeples, sun-drenched parks,
cobblestone streets. Glossy, idyllic.
Her face glows with pride. She's been traveling a week,
does not speak good English.
Carries these pictures to show.

Why have you come to New Zealand?
Marina's question.

    To see beautiful land
    like in pictures
    it is my dream.

Then your dream has come true.

Sonja's smile
uncertain.

Marina shows us pictures in an album.
Her little sons, faces impish.
Her wedding to Daniel, hand in hand in the garden,
a garland of white flowers around her head.
Snapshot of two men
floating on tubes in the lily pond,
naked butt cheeks like gleaming quarters.

Why have you come? My question.
Marina smiles. *It was my dream.*
Her eyes, blue and bottomless.
Shadows skim below the surface.

VI

We turn potato beds
Pound potato beds
Marina's shovel
rhythmic
clay chunks
broken apart
with each blow
we are sweating
at last
ground lies still.

NAVIGATING CUSTOMS

VII

Jacob, Marina's youngest, half-Maori but fair like her. Bullied at school by bigger boys. Willful teen, stole tractor parts from neighboring farms. Disappeared for days, smoked dope, spoke little. The music he listened to, so bloodcurdling it made her sick.

One night, she told us, hurricane swept the hills. Winds howled. Hail rattled the buildings. Jacob cowered in bed. His window shattered. Blanket lifted, hovered over him like a ghost. He screamed. In the morning, fallen trees. He was shaken and subdued. See what you've brought upon yourself? I told you that music draws bad energy to you. She was teasing. Later, she found him smashing his cassettes to bits.

VIII

I repot seedlings in Marina's greenhouse.
Young lettuce, stalks limp spines.
I worry for them. Work slowly, meticulous,
pat the earth around their roots
like I am dressing a wound.
Haven't you finished? Marina takes over for me,
not with impatience, just the desire to see things done.

I knew nothing when I came.
How did you learn?
I just had to.

Night. Crunching leaves, flashlight in hand
I descend into bush. Outhouse door a burlap curtain.
Cold seat. Something furred
brushes my leg. A gasp
sharp as a knife in my chest.
In the beam of my flashlight
cat's black tail flickers out of view.

Holly and I sleep in Jacob's old room.
This place shifts and ebbs,
a shore in flux with the tide.
Top bunk, spider gazes down at me from the rafters.
Drum of my heart growing fainter, tide receding,
I am driftwood.

IX

Sometimes, without warning, Holly's stories of home pour out. Her face grows flushed, alive *meeting this guy in the middle of bloody nowhere pitch black couldn't see a damned thing out there two in the morning driver thought I was off my rocker* we listen, spurred, try to reply, keep something afloat. The torrent subsides and she falls silent again.

NAVIGATING CUSTOMS

Talia Weisz

X

A favorite question: where are you from? Born in Montréal, my mother in St. Louis, her mother in a Russian *shtetl*. I can't find it on the map. 1916. My grandmother boarded a cattle ship, ten years old. Jacob, her father, already in America. She'd forgotten him. *He's a rich man now, a famous baker.* Dignified, in a black top hat. Hordes spilling into open air, endless lines of people. Pale faces, she didn't want to strip, hands poked her, cacophony of voices, her youngest sister sobbing. She finally saw him running towards them, a stranger. Shoes worn, apron dusty with flour. Her disappointment: a stone plummeting inside her. It hit bottom and shattered. The pieces washed away, seeds re-rooting.

XI

I search the map for Hawaiki.
No one's sure where it was.
Around Tahiti, some say Peru.
The past, a gaping chasm. What falls in is lost.
Do not lean too far over the edge.

XII

My mother
once dreamed
the sea into our backyard.
Through the dining room window
she saw across to the horizon.

Whale surfaced
in the distance
came closer
body sleek.
It crashed
through the window
flood of water

I awake drenched.
sleeping bag twisted
night still
cows mooing
they've escaped
from the neighbouring farm
trampled Marina's field.

In the morning, we set out in gumboots
to repair the damage, flatten holes in the mud.
Squish of our boots. Up ahead,
Marina's tall figure, a stake driven into the earth.

People come here with romantic notions.
But Hokianga is a mirror. It exposes you.

NAVIGATING CUSTOMS

Talia Weisz

XIII

Tom is Marina's neighbour,
pleasant fellow, a Scot, white hair, gangly as a teen.
Been here nearly as long as she has,
rents the old caravan on the edge of her land,
empty since the last of her children have gone.
Painted letters above the door. *Jacob*
my brother's middle name.

Tom leads Sonja and me up a path into the hills
into the bush, shimmering leaves, shafts of light,
branches like spines.
Sound of our breathing, forest breathing.
We stop. A sheltered clearing.
A tree, enormous, rooted not once but twice.
Must've fallen over in a gale.
One set of roots half unearthed,
the tree prostrate, its branches reach up,
leaves catching the sun.
Grew another set from its trunk.

Sonja and I stay. She sketches the tree,
I sketch her sketching it.
I mail the drawing home. Forget to address it.

THE MEDICINE WOMAN OF BUTARITARI (CONT'D)
BY CLEO PASKAL

Cleo Paskal's *varied print, radio, television and film assignments have taken her from Timbuktu to the Largest Ball of Twine in Minnesota. In the past six years, Paskal has won fourteen major writing awards, including Grand Prize (best entry overall) from the North American Travel Journalist's Association (twice).*

There was also another price she would be expected to pay. The Caller Of Dolphins always died young and, when she died, she could not be buried on the island. Just off the coast of Butaritari there was a dark blot on the turquoise ocean, a bottomless hole in the sea floor that, it was believed, led down into the home of the dolphins.

The body of the Caller Of Dolphins was brought to this spot and placed in the water. Other bodies would have just floated away, but hers sunk, down, down, reuniting her again and forever with the dolphins, who were always happy to have company.

And that sacrifice, dying young and being separated forever from her family, the Caller Of Dolphins was willing to make for the honour of being able to provide food for her hungry Island.

And that is the end of The Story.

Winnie looks rather pointedly at the now cold dish of roasted swamp taro.

Brushing away the flies that aren't already embedded and struggling in the beige mass, I start munching away dutifully.

"But Winnie, is that true? Do they still Call The Dolphins?"

"The last time the dolphins were Called was about thirty years ago. I had just had my first child, so I couldn't swim with them. I watched, though... You know, my husband's family is one of the two who can Call. I asked my sister-in-law why she won't do it. She says she doesn't want to die young. I told her it's too late anyway since she is already in her sixties but she still won't do it. I guess she prefers the safer honour of buying the whole island tins of corned beef."

Night comes and it is time for Winnie to stop talking. She sucks on her last cigarette, making the tip come alive, then stubs it out and goes to sleep beside me. The waves rumble and the insects chatter. But there is no voice to keep me. I can't even hear Winnie breathing. I feel crushingly alone.

I can't sleep. My fever is rising. I can feel it. I am prone to anaphylactic reactions to viruses. This means a simple cold, allowed to run rampant, could very near kill me. Winnie is treating whatever it is I caught but not the allergy. I hadn't expected it to get so bad. The reaction is easy to prevent with some antihistamines and adrenaline, but Winnie had said I wasn't to take any western medicine, as it could combine with what she has given me and make me worse.

So I lie there, my adrenaline and antihistamines at the foot of my bed, my fever climbing. I feel the weight on my chest getting heavier, each breath a conscious effort. It is so hard, so hopeless. Tears trickle down my temples. I am too exhausted to sob, so the tears mix silently with my sweat and slowly evaporate in the stifling heat.

The sticky river of tears on my cheeks terrifies me. It comes from deep within. I hadn't realized I felt so powerless, so despairing. I am dying. My body knows I am dying. I am paralyzed by a desire to do nothing. Just wait. Just float away on my fever. But my tears scare me.

I drag myself towards the antihistamines and adrenaline, tears coming faster, soul stretching. I fumble with my bag as though underwater, desperately frustrated by my weakness and lack of control. Finding an antihistamine, I choke it down. It scrapes my throat like a pebble and makes me nauseous.

The adrenaline is an inhalant. I find it and pause. It is very strong. If anything is going to react with Winnie's medicine, it will be a shot of pure adrenaline. I am overwhelmed by sadness, by loneliness. There is no one to decide for me. No one to ask. It is so quiet.

I concentrate all my energy and depress the adrenaline while breathing in as deeply as I can. Depleted, I drop the dispenser to the floor. For a few seconds, I feel no different. Then I pass out.

I awake suddenly. Morning. I ache and am weak. But Winnie is there, fussing around the room. I smile. When she sees my open eyes, she comes over and feels my head and abdomen. "Hmmmmm."

"The medicine I have been giving you isn't strong enough," she says. And she leaves.

Alone, I do a mental inventory. I am all here but my fever is still high and I feel like a flickering shadow.

Winnie returns with a new and improved set of twigs. She scrapes together a new concoction for me to drink and I dutifully down it. Almost immediately I start to feel immeasurably worse. Within a half-an-hour I am completely incapacitated by a crippling headache.

"Winnie," I moan, "are you trying to kill me?"

Winnie patiently explains that if the first dose of medicine doesn't work after two days, she creates a stronger brew. With western medicine, she says, the goal is often to suppress symptoms until the body heals itself. With local medicine, the goal is to bring out all the disease at once and get it over with quickly. The original "what doesn't kill you makes you stronger."

Well, I am certainly getting sicker, which, as Winnie keeps cheerfully telling me, is a good thing. For several hellish hours, I just groan self-pityingly. Then, I start to fell better. By the afternoon, I am stronger. By the evening, I am practically perky. The days of being sick have left me physically exhausted. For the first night since I arrived on Butaritari, I sleep well.

I wake up nearly refreshed. Winnie proffers another dose of extra strength medicine. I have my doubts but she explains that the medicine just amplified existing symptoms, so if I am feeling better, it won't make me as sick as I had been the day before. I drink it and the effects are barely perceptible.

Around mid-day, the missing nurse staggers in, looking terrible. He is holding something I hadn't seen since arriving on the atoll. Forms. The sight of them makes me feel sick again. My illness and convalescence has taken place wholly outside the realm of institutions and paperwork and labeling and bureaucracy. Now this man wants to tag me and file me away in the hospital on Tarawa. And, for bureaucratic reasons, I have no choice but to agree. I have to end my trip and go home.

It takes several days to reach the pertinent authorities in Tarawa by citizen band radio, but within hours of reaching them, it is announced on Radio Kiribati that the country's only plane will come to Butaritari the following morning to pick me up. Winnie doesn't have a radio. The neighbour's boys are sent to tell her.

Winnie tells me it will take at least a couple of months for me to get up to full strength. She feeds me one last dose of special tea before I fly off. It is starting to taste good.

The plane arrives unexpectedly. There is no time for a proper good-bye. Winnie's nephew, a school teacher, abandons his class to a visiting missionary and drives me to the airport on the back of his moped, using up a large part of his difficult-to-get petrol ration.

The plane takes me (and a load of bananas) back to Tarawa. From the airport, a van delivers me to the country's only hospital. It is staffed primarily by two competent, well-meaning, Estonian U.N. doctors with no training whatsoever in tropical medicine.

One of them declares I have dengue fever, an illness for which western medicine has no known treatment. I rather doubt it, but I needed a label. So, dengue fever it is.

The hospital stay is surprising. I miss Winnie terribly, but my welcome is warm. Everyone seems to know who I am – they look me in the eyes, and smile. It takes a while for my addled brain to figure it out. The Radio Kiribati announcement has made me a part of I-Kiribati society. Now they know what is cooking in my pot.

As a result, when I walk the streets after being released from the hospital, I have the all-embracing comfort of having stranger after stranger nod to me, knowingly. And, as I listened to Radio Kiribati during my convalescence, I can nod back.

But what I am really listening for is news of Winnie and her island of terrible magic and endless wonder. It doesn't come. The dream is over.